IF YOU FIND ME...

by

DONNA B. MACDONALD

IF YOU FIND ME...

BY

DONNA B. MACDONALD

INFINITY
PUBLISHING

Copyright © 2010 by Sue A. Owings

The photograph on the cover is Plum Island, Massachusetts, taken by the author, Donna MacDonald, in 1979.

ISBN 0-7414-6260-5

Printed in the United States of America

Published November 2010

∞

INFINITY PUBLISHING
1094 New DeHaven Street, Suite 100
West Conshohocken, PA 19428-2713
Toll-free (877) BUY BOOK
Local Phone (610) 941-9999
Fax (610) 941-9959
Info@buybooksontheweb.com
www.buybooksontheweb.com

DEDICATION

Life writes a story in our hearts.
In it we find splendor and beauty,
the thrills of fun and adventure,
the depths of sadness and
the heights of joy.
And through it all, Love.

We find the fountain of strength
and the shield of resilience.
Which is good because we learn
adversity doesn't come sugar-coated.

We learn that when it comes
knocking on your door,
it's good to have those with you
who will help you deal with it,
stomp on it or send it packing.

I am blessed to have the best.
So I dedicate my book to those who help me
deal with it every day –

***To my dear Mom, Ruth,
and my good buddy, Sue.***

PROLOGUE

White flakes fell steadily from a gray-clouded sky. Cassie swiped her red woolen mitten across her face. Unfortunately, the mitten was already soaking wet from the constant snowfall. It chilled her face. Shivering, Cassie fumbled with the collar of her peacoat, finally pulling it up around her neck.

"So, Cassie, seeings how neither one of us has a date for this Saturday, shall we go to the school dance together?" Bobbie asked, her breath hanging in foggy clouds. The girls were dressed nearly identical. You could tell them apart because Bobbie, small and compact, had long brown hair with waves and frizz. They were the classic female Mutt and Jeff. With her height and build, Cassie could have been Twiggy's sister, including her pixie-cut hair plastered to her face.

Bobbie had recently turned eighteen and Cassie's eighteenth would be in June. The girls had been best friends forever and they'd finally reached their senior year. Soon they would decide which college they were going to attend together. But right now Cassie had to face up to something and she dreaded it.

How to say it? Blurt it out? Lying would never cross her mind. The teenager ranked honesty right up there with the commandments and the golden rule.

Cassie took a deep breath. "I have to run something by you, Bobbie. You see, I got asked yesterday but you won't like who was doing the asking."

"Silly. You could go with just about anybody. I wouldn't mind. Except for Lenny Marek, of course. But that goes without saying, right?"

Cassie pursed her frozen lips. Her mind zigzagged everywhere but the subject at hand. Suddenly her peacoat, sodden from the snow, weighed heavily on her shoulders. The sky had turned a dirty pewter and the snow fell faster, fueled by the wind.

Realizing that Cassie hadn't agreed with her, Bobbie stopped in her tracks, grabbing Cassie's arm.

"Tell me it isn't so, Cass," Bobbie said in a low, biting voice.

"You never told me why you broke up with him," she plaintively answered.

"WHAT DIFFERENCE DOES IT MAKE???" Bobbie screamed at the top of her lungs. "I dumped him. Don't you think I had a very good reason for

IF YOU FIND ME...

doing that? This is like some kind of betrayal."
Shaking her head, Bobbie mumbled over and over,
"I can't believe this."

"I didn't say yes. Honest," Cassie pleaded.

"Yeah, but you didn't say no either, right?"
Bobbie practically whispered, making Cassie move
her head closer to hear. "The guy is a CREEP. A
lousy degenerate creep. OKAY?" Her cheeks,
already pink from the cold, turned flaming red.
"Stay away from him. Far away, got it?"

"Oh geez. Did the guy do something, Bobbie?"

"Not exactly, but not for want of trying."

"I'm so sorry. I didn't know. Of course I'll tell
the jerk where to go."

"A little late, Cassie. You should've said no just
on principle. Know what I mean?" Bobbie started
trudging away in the snow.

"Wait up," Cassie called, struggling after her in
the wind and snow.

"Just leave me alone, okay?"

"Oh come on, Bobbie. Give me another chance.
I screwed up. I'm sorry. We've been friends since
kindergarten. You can forgive me, can't you?"

"I dunno," Bobbie answered. "Maybe. But not
today."

"Hey, hold on. We ought to at least walk
together the rest of the way home. This snowstorm
is getting worse." Bobbie didn't answer and Cassie
was left to follow a few steps behind.

3

Breathing hard against the wind and blowing wet snow, Cassie struggled. Bobbie got further and further ahead. Cassie was the brainiac, she edited the school newspaper and wrote several of the columns each month, while Bobbie was the athlete of the duo, captain of the softball team and a gymnastics star as well. So it didn't surprise Cassie too much when she lost sight of her friend. Visibility had dropped to about twenty feet. The few cars on the road inched along, even those with tire chains.

Eventually she came up to Bobbie's house, but didn't see anyone. A pristine field of snow lay across the front walk. "That's odd. Bobbie couldn't have been that far ahead of me. Where are her footprints?" Cassie wondered. "Even if they got covered over, there should still be a depression or something." Then she thought about the backdoor, but there were no footprints in the snow leading down the driveway to the backdoor either. Cassie was bothered by the puzzle but the freezing cold trumped her curiosity. A few more steps brought her to the corner.

Almost home. Suddenly though, her foot sank deep in the snow, catching the edge of the curb that lay hidden beneath. Down she went, face first in the snowbank. The new snow, only six inches deep, covered a foot of hard snow and ice, left by last week's snowstorm. Trying to rub her sore elbow through the thick jacket proved useless so Cassie brushed herself off and continued the difficult walk home. Someone had shoveled a path up the driveway. Wearily she trudged the last few feet, encouraged by the shining lights inside. She couldn't wait to get into the warmth and coziness of their home, out of the freezing storm.

By the time Cassie walked through the backdoor, she was frozen to the bone. Shivering, she put her arms behind her, letting the heavy wet jacket slide off her arms onto the floor. Before Gram could come along and say something, she took it and put it on the back of a kitchen chair, shoving the chair over next to the radiator. Just about to walk away, Cassie suddenly turned back to check the radiator, making sure it was giving off heat. At least once or twice a week the old furnace in the cellar clunked out and the radiators turned cold faster than her brother could polish off a bowl of ice cream. For now, the old radiator was cranking out the heat.

"Oh hi, honey. I'm glad you're home. They should've sent the kids home early today. It looks frightful out there." Gram walked up, throwing her arms around her granddaughter in a big hug. "Cassandra, you're freezing!" Gram rubbed her hands up and down Cassie's arms to bring up some warmth. Cassie flinched at her Grandmother's touch. "Cassie, what happened? Are you hurt?"

"I fell on the sidewalk. It's so slippery out there. My elbow and ankle both hurt but I'm sure it's nothing."

"You go on up and get out of those wet clothes. I'll get a bucket of hot water and epsom salts going so you can soak your ankle. And I'm sure some hot chocolate and fresh baked chocolate chip cookies will make things a whole lot better, don't you think?"

"Sounds wonderful, Gram." Cassie's skirt was soaked and her nylon-clad legs had turned purple. "I'm so cold, I don't think the circulation is ever going to start up again in my legs. You know, Gram, I think all the girls in my school should protest. We ought to all decide to wear pants to school one day in protest of the girls' dress code. Having to wear skirts and nylons in the winter is a travesty."

"Good word, Cassie, 'travesty.' I like it. Should be good in a scrabble game, don't you think?"

"Grams I'm serious. And it's probably too long to be useful in the game. ANYWAY," she continued theatrically, "if they checked attendance records, I'm sure they'd find that there are more girls absent in winter than boys because girls get more colds thanks to the stupid way we have to dress."

"I agree, dear. Girl Power!" Gram yelled.

Cassie shook her head. Her grandmother often made her laugh.

"At the very least you should write an editorial about it for the school paper," Gram shouted as Cassie limped up the stairs.

It felt as if she was never going to get warm. Midnight was curled up on the thick quilt of Cassie's bed. The black kitty opened one eye and flicked an ear.

"That the best hello you can muster?" Cassie asked her. "C'mere you." She scooped the huge Midnight up in her arms and hugged her close to her chest. "Ooh, you are so nice and warm." Midnight yawned and began purring. She was a laid back cat who enjoyed loving every chance she got. Reluctantly putting her down, Cassie sat on the edge of the bed and struggled out of her panty hose. "I'm glad these things were invented, Middy. Although right now they are sticking to me like glue. But then, a year ago I'd be unhooking a garter belt and nylons." Cassie sighed. She really did wish the girls could wear pants, at least in winter.

By the time Cassie finished dressing in warm pants, turtleneck and sweatshirt, the phone rang. One thing about her Dad, he was handy. He could do just about anything. One day he came home with a bunch of old phones and lines and proceeded to hook up phone lines in almost everyone's room. Of course they were all of the same phone number, but Cassie didn't care. She had a phone in her own room. At night she and Bobbie could talk for hours while Cassie laid on her bed. Bobbie had a phone in her bedroom, too, and she even had a different phone number than the rest of her family. The Avery's were quite well off. Amazing that the "rich" neighborhood lay a street corner away.

Didn't matter to Cassie, though. She had a Mom and Dad who totally loved her and her brother, and Grams who was the best. Occasionally, Cassie wished her Mom didn't have to work a full time job, but she understood that the family needed the money. Nope, she wouldn't trade places with her best friend for anything. Sure, Mrs. Avery didn't work, but that didn't mean she was around much – she belonged to so many organizations and at times Bobbie complained that the 'club ladies' got more of her mother's attention than she did. The ringing phone caught her attention. Maybe it was Bobbie, ready to talk to her again. Cassie hoped so, she didn't want to leave things the way they were.

But when she picked up, the last person she would have expected to hear from was Jack Avery, Bobbie's older brother. Jackson Avery was a senior at Emerson College in Boston. With his long hair, Jack had happily embraced the hippie culture, much to his uptight Boston blue-blooded parents' chagrin.

But Jack was clearly agitated. "Is Bobbie over there with you?" His words were running so fast together, Cassie could barely catch them.

"No. She didn't come over. Actually we kind of

had a disagreement on the way home from school. Bobbie went on ahead of me and I couldn't catch up. I lost sight of her."

"She's missing," Jack was telling her over and over. "Bobbie's missing. She came home, changed her clothes and grabbed $200 from Mom's Mad Money jar."

"Wow. No way, Jack. Absolutely not. Don't tell me Bobbie stole $200 and took off. Come on, where would she go? In case you haven't noticed, there's a snowstorm blowing outside – just a few flakes short of a nor'easter blizzard. Know what I mean?" Cassie got up and started pacing the worn linoleum floor. She'd been saving her money to buy a rug for her floor – to make it warmer, she'd told her folks. "Oh Jack, she must be freezing out there."

"It's more likely that someone picked her up in a car," he said. Although Jack hesitated a minute, he asked, "Are you sure you didn't know about this?"

"No!" Cassie shouted. "If I had any idea at all, I would have talked her out of whatever it is."

"Well, any ideas who she could be with? Who might have picked her up?" Jack pleaded.

Cassie did have one idea, but it was too absurd, really, to suggest it. She had to make a phone call first. "Not really. Besides, I didn't see any familiar cars going by when I was walking, but I suppose it could have come from the other direction and gone back that way. I still find it hard to believe. And

Jack, I don't get how she could've gotten into the house. There were absolutely no footprints in the snow on your front walk or leading up to the backdoor. I checked, because I was close enough behind Bobbie that I thought I might catch her just going up the steps. It was like she disappeared -- before she even got home."

Jack coughed. "Um, look, ... well, I have to go. The police are here now and mother just got home, too. I'll let you know if we hear anything." Jack hung up abruptly, not waiting for Cassie's reply.

"Whoa, that was distinctly odd, Middy." Tiny prickles jumped up and down her spine. "Something isn't right." But even more importantly, "WHERE IS BOBBIE?"

Hysteria wasn't far off, Cassie realized. "I've got to get over there."

Cassie groaned. She and Mrs. Avery did not mix well. But for Bobbie's sake, she'd do just about anything.

Cassie gave it some thought as she sat on the bed again, stroking Midnight. Her presence was hypnotic and calming. Pretty soon her thoughts returned to part of their conversation. Who might have picked her up?

"It did seem as if Bobbie avoided telling me much about Lenny. What if... what if they're actually still seeing each other? But then, why would he have invited me to the dance?"

IF YOU FIND ME...

"Mrruph," Midnight answered. Cassie looked at her wise kitty. Green eyes stared up at her, willing her to figure it out. "To make Bobbie jealous. Of course. I tell Bobbie, and she gets steamed and goes to him. Ok, smarty cat, but Bobbie just learned about it on our walk home. What do you say to that."

Midnight stretched out her black paw, touching Cassie's leg, with just a tiny bit of disdain in her twitching whiskers.

"Well, yeah, I did see them talking together in the hallway, on the way to our last classes. Oh crap. It's all a set up, isn't it. He asks me out. People think the two of them are done with each other. They arrange for him to pick her up, but we always walk home together and she has to figure out how to get rid of me so I don't see her go off with him or something like that. Or my wild imagination just took a giant leap and I'm so far off track I'm going to sound like a complete idiot if I tell this to anyone." Cassie took a deep breath. "First things first. Call Lenny and see if he's home." Middy started purring.

"Okay then. Here goes," she said, dialing Lenny Marek's phone number.

"Uh, hi Mrs. Marek. This is Cassie Wood. Can I please speak to Lenny?"

"Well, I'm sorry dear, but he's not here. He took his car out about a half hour ago. I tried to stop him,

11

but he said it was urgent. At least he has snow tires. Fat lot of good that will do him if he hits ice."

Mama Marek, motor mouth, Cassie remembered. She had to interrupt or Mrs. Marek would go on forever.

"Mrs. Marek, did he say he was meeting someone?"

"No, he just said he really had to go. I think to help someone out of a jam, now that you mention it."

"Did you happen to notice if he was carrying anything with him?"

Mrs. Marek must have been thinking, she was actually quiet for a few seconds. "Well, I'm not positive but I thought I saw his backpack." But now she was getting suspicious about all the questions. "Just what is this about, Cassie?" she asked warily. "Has something happened?"

Cassie could hear the worry in her voice. She had no idea if it would help Bobbie to say something or make things worse. What to do? The overriding thought at the moment is whether or not Bobbie is safe, she decided, and no one could know that unless they could find her. Maybe the more people that know, the quicker we can find her.

"It's about Roberta Avery, Mam. She's missing."

"What? Oh Lordy sakes. Are you sure?"

Cassie replied, "I was told that the police are

over at her house now and they're going to start searching."

"Oh my dear. It will be so difficult with this storm. Listen, if I hear from Lenny or he comes back, I'll tell him. I'm sure he'll want to help."

"Yes, of course. Please, just one more thing? Do you happen to know if he and Bobbie had been in touch recently?"

Mrs. Marek laughed. "Honey, let me ask you something. At the end of the day, do your parents know everyone you've spoken to and seen that day?"

"Oh, I see what you mean."

"And believe me, it's even worse with teenage boys."

After they hung up Cassie quickly grabbed her snow boots out of the closet and her winter jacket with the fur on the hood. She also grabbed her CSB – crime-solving bag. It was a hobby – finding lost cats, things that go missing from peoples' yards or kids' bikes, the neighbors might call the cops but they'd probably call Cassie first. She was getting a reputation for helping out in these situations. It was her dream to go into some type of investigative work. But she never thought that one day her best friend would be the one to go missing.

Looking out her snow covered window, Cassie fought the urge to swear. The gray afternoon was being swiftly taken over by oncoming darkness. "Darn this snowstorm," she screamed in frustration.

"Too soon to be dark. Too soon," she whispered desperately to Middy. "We have to find her."

Cassie limped down the stairs as fast as her boot-clad feet would allow. Wafting from the kitchen came the smell of hot chocolate and fresh baked cookies. Cassie groaned. She would love to stay and eat with Gram.

"Sorry, Grams, can't stop for hot chocolate." Cassie explained about Jack's phone call. "So, I can't figure out if she's missing or if she and Lenny have just gone off together for the afternoon. It doesn't make sense. And I totally don't believe Jack's statement that she took $200 of her mother's money. That just isn't Bobbie."

Ginny Barton sipped her hot drink. "I agree, Cassie. But what I find odd is that Bea Avery,…"

Cassie interrupted her grandmother. "Uh, uh, Grams. BEATRICE Avery, remember? Last time you called her Bea she had a conniption fit. MY NAME IS BEATRICE. PLEASE REMEMBER THAT, MADAM." Cassie shook her head.

"So true, dear, so true. I feel sorry for the woman, to tell you the truth."

"What? Why on earth would you feel sorry for someone like that?" Cassie asked.

"When you say, someone like 'that,' what do you mean exactly?"

"Well, she has everything. A fancy house, a good husband…"

This time it was her grandmother who interrupted. "And how do you know he's a good husband?"

Cassie unzipped her jacket while she thought a minute. "I guess I don't know for sure. But he has a good job and they seem to have every comfort one could want. She doesn't have to work – she can just goof off and do anything she likes."

"Do I detect a hint of bitterness in your voice, dear?"

"No, not really. I know she does a lot of committee work on various community projects, but it doesn't seem like she's ever a part of actually doing something. Do you know what I mean, Gram? And she NEVER looks like she's enjoying anything. I guess you're right, that is kind of sad."

"I think so. And remember, too, that some people put on airs and do busy work to cover how unhappy they really are."

"Whoa. You really think so? I mean, you think that Mrs. Avery deep down could be an unhappy person?"

"Actually, I do. I'm sure of it. But there isn't time now for us to talk about it. Instead, why don't you tell me exactly what you think you're going to do by going over there right now." Gram's voice was soft, yet deep, an unusual quality for a woman. Cassie loved hearing her talk.

She told her grandmother about the experiment

she was going to perform in the front yard, then inform the officer at the Avery's house of the results. "I think it's going to be interesting."

"Cassie, you probably shouldn't be walking on that ankle that you injured. Can't you take a few minutes and at least soak it first?"

Cassie zipped up her jacket. "I promise, Gram, as soon as I can I'll get back here and soak it and give it a rest. But right now finding Bobbie is way more important." Grabbing her CSB, Cassie headed out the back door. The snow was still coming down. It seemed to be falling more rapidly than when she had walked home. It might skew the results, but Cassie felt she had to try. Finding a patch of undisturbed snow, she painfully tromped up and down in it leaving several footprints. Obviously, conditions were different here than at Bobbie's house, but she couldn't see herself doing this over there where Mrs. Avery and everyone else would probably be watching.

Next she pulled her stopwatch out of her crime-solving bag and started it. The purpose was to see how much time it would take for the footprints to be completely filled in, not leaving any noticeable sign. At the fifteen minute mark Cassie gave up. They were about half-way filled with snow. She knew for a fact that after Bobbie had left her, Cassie had walked for about eight minutes before reaching Bobbie's house. So in those eight minutes, any footsteps Bobbie made at her house would still have been visible by the time Cassie walked by. Bobbie never entered her house. That was now a fact. Heaving a deep sigh, Cassie decided it was time to talk to Jack. And it had better be alone.

Cassie thought about taking the short cut, the path that wound around behind their garage to eventually land at Bobbie's backdoor but one look at the snow-covered bushes scrapping against the side of the garage nixed that idea. She'd like to stay dry for a little while, at least.

Instead Cassie tromped through snow approaching knee-high depth. Around the corner and following the deeply covered sidewalk Cassie made it without mishap. Her injured ankle was now numb with cold and she figured that was probably a darn good thing.

Mulling over again that unsettling phone call from Jack, Cassie felt the utmost urgency to talk to him and get to the bottom of this whole affair. Wind-swept snow chilled her face. Cassie thought, we *must* find Bobbie.

A uniformed police officer stood outside on the Avery's porch.

"Hello, officer," she called, walking up the front walk.

"Who are you?" he asked with a chill as biting as the winter air assaulting her cold face.

"I'm Cassandra Wood, Roberta Avery's best

friend. I got a call from her brother about fifteen minutes ago. He said Bobbie was missing and that the house had been robbed. Is it true?" she asked breathless from the cold feeling in her heart.

Mrs. Avery poked her head out the door. "Cassandra, where is Roberta?" she demanded. Mrs. Avery turned to the policeman. "Officer, make her tell me where my daughter is right now!"

"I don't know, Mrs. Avery, honest. If I did, I'd tell you, of course." Cassie limped up onto the small front porch.

"You're lying!" she shouted. Cassie was surprised to see the woman's face turning purple. "You're her best friend," she screamed, pointing her index finger close to Cassie's right eye. "You tell us this instant. Or this officer will arrest you!"

"Please calm down, Mrs. Avery." The officer tried to calm the hysterical woman.

"Mrs. Avery, why on earth would you think I had anything to do with Bobbie's disappearance?"

"Don't call her that! Don't you dare call her that. Her name is Roberta Grace. You and your people are so déclassé." Beatrice, as Cassie thought of her at this moment, turned to the officer. "She is the last one to have seen my daughter. Take her downtown and make her tell you what's happened." When the officer didn't reply, she shouted, "RIGHT NOW!"

At that tumultuous moment, Jack showed up.

Relieved, Cassie looked to him for the voice of reason. Of course, Jack could be stoned. He'd taken to using pot not long ago, but Cassie figured Jack on marijuana had to be better than Mrs. Avery who was obviously short a few pills of valium at the moment. Pour the whole bottle down her, Cassie thought.

Jack ushered everybody back inside the house, while the officer brought Jack up to date. Then Cassie explained about their walk home. Mrs. Avery, of course, didn't believe a word of it. And she pointed to Cassie's limp.

"See, look at that! Cassandra's hurt. Obviously, she and my daughter had a fight and this tramp has done something awful to my little girl!"

"Mrs. Avery, I slipped on the sidewalk and injured my ankle. Bobbie and I had a disagreement but I assure you she was fine when she went on ahead of me. I have no idea what happened in those eight minutes."

"Look, she hasn't been missing that long," the officer said, trying to diffuse the heated discussion. "We can't even call in a missing person report on her yet. Why don't you call her friends, the hospital and anyone else you can think of to see who else might have seen her."

Jack answered, "I already did all that. No sign of her in the emergency room of Melrose or Woburn hospitals, or the New England Sanitarium.

Those are the only ones around. And none of her friends have heard from her. Their only suggestions were either Cassie here or Lenny Marek, her last boyfriend."

"I talked to Lenny's Mom and she claims that he's out helping a friend. He took his car," Cassie added.

"Okay, that's a place we can begin. May I use your phone?" he asked Mrs. Avery, who had been standing in stony silence so long that Cassie was beginning to wonder if she'd had a fit of some kind that rendered her suddenly mute. Maybe all that yelling took away her voice. Yeah, right, Cassie thought, like that's going to happen.

Jack whispered something to his mother and she left the room.

While the officer was on the phone, Cassie asked Jack, "So what was the magical phrase that got her to leave the room?"

"That's easy. I told her it was time for her medication. Valium of the day, of course."

"Thank goodness. She was wound so tight I thought she was going to go into orbit."

Jack motioned her to sit in one of the living room chairs.

"You can talk to me, Jack, can't you? What's really going on?"

Jack rubbed his hands together over and over. He kept clearing his throat.

"Don't even think about lying to me, Jack. Those little nervous signs of yours? They tell me you're lying. Don't do it, okay? She's my best friend. I'm really worried."

Jack noticed the curious little tremor in Cassie's lower lip. He felt a knot tightening in his stomach and a tiny stab hit his heart. "There's nothing I can tell you."

Cassie realized from the pleading in Jack's voice and the anguish settling on his face, that he was truly concerned. But she also knew he wasn't being up front with her.

"Tell me this. Did you take the money so you can buy pot?"

Jack jumped off the couch and towered over her. "Absolutely not!"

Finally, Cassie thought, a truthful answer. But it didn't help further the investigation. "How could Bobbie have taken the money when she never walked into the house this afternoon? Can you answer me that?"

Heaving a huge sigh, Jack reached down for Cassie's hand. "Come with me, we can't talk about this out in the open." After checking that his mother was in the kitchen with the policeman – she appeared to be making him a cup of coffee, no less – Jack led Cassie upstairs to Bobbie's bedroom.

"You're right about one thing. I took the money. But it's not what you think. Cassie, I can honestly tell you that I have no idea where Bobbie is. She asked me to get the money for her yesterday. She wouldn't tell me why. I SWEAR to you, I have no idea what's happened to my sister." Jack ran his hand through his hair. He wore it long and loose down over his shirt collar. His face, framed by his black hair, seemed even paler than usual.

Cassie casually looked over the top of Bobbie's desk. Nothing stood out. Nothing said, *"I've gone, come and find me here."*

"She's my best friend. How could I not know that there was something going on with her? I don't understand." Cassie kept shaking her head. "Don't you think you should tell the police about this?"

Gingerly, Jack sat on the bed. A pink bedspread covered with gardens of flowers, so many bright and beautiful colors, seemed out of place with Bobbie missing. It was too bright. Too normal.

Music floated in from Jack's bedroom. He must have left his radio on. The new hit by Barry Maguire rang out in the silence, "Eve of Destruction." Cassie shivered as the dire warnings bellowed across the airwaves.

Jack lowered his head. "I don't know about telling the cops. If Bobbie is okay would she want me to? The money seems to imply that she planned this, doesn't it? That she needed it for something?"

"Could she have owed it to someone? Or had to pay someone off because they know something?"

Even to Cassie this sounded far-fetched. "This is ridiculous." Cassie looked down at the desk again.

Jack saw her gaze. "Go ahead and look through her desk. If anyone could figure what she needed money for, you could. You know her best."

"Do I, Jack? I'm beginning to wonder if any of us know her at all."

Cassie pawed through papers and folders, one of which was marked, "CAR." She opened it. There were a few clippings from the newspaper – cars for sale -- section. "This looks to be from last Sunday's Boston Globe. She's circled one about a 1957 Chevy – good condition – $200." Picking it up, Cassie waved it at Jack. "This could be it! She took the money to buy this car. Oh my gosh, what if the guy came by with the car and picked her up so she could try it. We have to show this to the police!"

Cassie and Jack ran down the stairs and into the kitchen. A much more mellow Mrs. Avery greeted them.

"Children, slow down. What on earth are you doing?"

"Officer...I'm sorry... what's your name?" Cassie asked.

"MacIntire. Brian MacIntire."

"Well, Officer MacIntire, take a look at this. It was on Bobbie's...excuse me... Roberta's desk." Cassie hoped that if she played by Beatrice's rules, maybe this mellower version of Mrs. Avery would let her stay while they figured this out.

"I don't recall giving you permission to go through my daughter's things," Mrs. A pointed out.

"It was me, Ma, I told her to do it. Cassie knows Bobbie as well as anyone and we need her help."

Cassie waited for an explosion but Mrs. Avery let it pass.

Meanwhile Officer MacIntire was on the phone with someone he called Sarge, giving him all the info about the car ad.

After hanging up he told them, "All right, this seems to be a good lead. And my colleagues are tracking down Lenny Marek to talk to him, too. I'll let you all know what we find out. In the meantime, if you hear anything be sure to let us know." Officer Mac turned to Mrs. Avery, his voice softened, "Officially she isn't missing, Mam, but let me assure you that the department is going all out. We aren't waiting. Because of the storm we know it could be dangerous for her out there wherever she is, but she could also be somewhere of her own choosing, somewhere safe. And the department is swamped. They tell me accidents are piling up from this weather. But we're doing our best. You can call anytime." Officer Mac handed her a business card, presumably with contact numbers.

And then he was gone. Quiet permeated the kitchen. Not even the refrigerator hummed. The void unsettled Cassie. Ominous things happen in total silence. And then there is no more quiet.

"All right, Cassie you might as well go home," Jack said.

Mrs. Avery stood up. "No, I think you were right, Jack." Mrs. Avery looked at Cassie with such sad brown eyes that Cassie thought she saw beads of tears forming in those little pools of dimming light. "Cassie, can you stay and go through Bobbie's room? See if you can come up with anything else that might tell us what's going on in her life." She hung her aristocratic head. It reminded Cassie of a champion horse she saw – he'd won race after race for years. But then one day it finally happened – he lost. That champion hung his head in sorrow. She'd seen it with her own eyes. The look of not measuring up when it counted. This horse had won countless races, a true champion. Then that one day he discovered, perhaps, that sometimes things happen, even when you try your best. Was Mrs. Avery feeling that way now? Wondering if she actually did her best? Was she wondering, *should I have tried harder to know my daughter?* Cassie hoped the woman wouldn't dwell on it, but instead put her energy into action helping to find out what happened to Bobbie.

CHAPTER ONE

She walked out of the dark, air conditioned coffee shop into the shimmering light. The air was a humid sea of heat. It felt like being underwater without an oxygen tank. Cassie groaned. She had to walk a block and a half back to her business.

Huffing and puffing, her hair ringing wet, Cassie finally pulled open the door into air conditioned relief. Earlier everyone had been complaining that the heat from the ovens and stoves took away all the coolness. But as Cassie plunked herself down in her chair, the slightly cooler air felt fabulous. Anything was better than the dripping heavy atmosphere outside.

Her assistant, Jane, had laid the newspaper open on her desk. Staring back at her was their new advertisement: "Cassie's Cuisine – Where Old Fashioned Cooking Tastes Even Better Than You Remember. Tired of reaching for antacids after you eat a fancy, spicy meal? Try Cassie's Cuisine for all your catering needs. Good bye heartburn. Hello

Delicious and Healthy. Let us help you serve a feast to your guests or a light luncheon for your meetings. And check out our Hearth Room or Conservatory for your tea party, birthday or small meeting event. Busy day with no time to cook? We can help with a full course meal for your family, delivered to your door, or a romantic repast. Cassie's Cuisine – catering to your needs." Placing the advertisement in the Cape Cod Times had been expensive, but hopefully, worth it.

She worried that the ad might have been too long but she wanted folks to know of their varied catering services. They weren't a big outfit but had slowly grown larger to where Cassie's Cuisine could now handle a one hundred person event – wedding, fundraiser, meeting, – you name it. The phone wasn't ringing off the hook these days, but it was hard to compete with the likes of Dorrie's Delectable Delights. Dorrie had a permanent staff of six, and a bunch of temps that came at her beck and call. Most of them young men. Dorrie's figure rivaled that of Raquel Welch or Jayne Mansfield, voluptuous and blonde, with a come-hither look. It was a mystery to Cassie how a girl like that could cook up such amazing food and present it with real style. Not exactly a feminist comment, Cassie realized, but truthful anyway. And Dorrie boasted that her company could cater to large scale events of two hundred or more. Personally, Cassie thought

Dorrie exaggerated her capabilities, and not just her company's.

"Knock, knock," Janie called as her small white knuckles rapped the open office door. "I see you found our ad. What do you think?"

"Looks great. Let's hope it catches a few eyes."

"Well, I don't want to burst your bubble, but I guess you didn't turn to the page before that one in the paper."

Cassie's eyebrows, a soft golden light-brown, so soft they looked like a baby's, reached up toward her bangs. Something told her from the sarcastic edge of Jane's voice, that Cassie was not going to like whatever she saw.

Sure enough a half-page ad stared back at her. Groaning, Cassie read, "Dorrie's Delectable Delights. We cater to your sophisticated palate. Your guests deserve the best. Weddings are one of our specialities. Choose from our delicious entrees such as succulent lobster baked in our sauce with seafood stuffing. And for your summer fundraising event we provide fresh vegetables grilled to perfection to accompany any of our buffct or cntrcc choices. For elegance and style call us at Dorrie's Delectable Delights. Call before June 30th to book your event with us and receive $25.00 off any order over $100."

"This is unbelievable," Janie complained, pacing the small office.

Cassie watched her friend, who would barely tip the scale to a hundred pounds soaking wet in her jeans, as she strutted angrily in the tiny space. It never occurred to her before, but Cassie marveled at the striking resemblance between Janie and her dear friend, Bobbie. *Don't go there. Don't let your mind wander back to that time of terror and anguish.*

"How did she know, Cassie?" Janie asked, bringing her back. Cassie couldn't help it. The past held Cassie in a grip so tight that she couldn't pry herself away from it. Not in all these years. *Listen to Jane. She needs you here.*

Janie was saying, "This is the first time we've put a big ad in the paper. Not only does she submit one bigger but it's even on the page before ours! I tell you, that witch has spies everywhere. That's how she knew."

Cassie laughed. The spell was broken. For now. "Listen to yourself," she told Jane. "You sound absolutely paranoid."

"C'mon, don't tell me it didn't occur to you, too. How many times this month has she scooped up a job that we gave a quote for and come in just under us? Hmm?"

Thinking, Cassie had to admit it happened on three different occasions. And yes, she did wonder last week when it happened for the third time, exactly how that could have been. Cassie's prices were much more reasonable than Dorrie's, at least on paper. So how *did* Dorrie know exactly what figure to offer so that it would come in just under theirs?

"Well, I can't believe anyone here could be telling Dorrie what prices we are offering. It's more likely she's heard about the jobs and called and asked the folks how much they've been quoted and then gave a better offer. It has to be that way."

"Okay, but that doesn't explain how she knew which jobs we were going to do before she came along and stole them out from under us." Janie had her hands on her small hips like she was scolding some errant terrier. That would be Dorrie all right. No, that would be unkind to the terrier, Cassie decided.

And besides, Janie had a point. A list of Cassie's employees went through her mind. She could eliminate herself and Janie and her grandmother. Grams wouldn't blab to folks would she? Maybe Cassie should check with her. And then there were the two high school girls, Bonnie and Jessica. They were working part-time for Cassie this summer. The girls had been conscientious at first when they started two weeks ago, but Jessica's enthusiasm seemed to be drooping a little since Cassie told her she couldn't have the 4th of July off, the day of the big Caterers' Cook-Off. Cassie was going to need everyone's help that day, including her Mom and Dad's. The only other employees were her cousin, Kevin, and his friend Tim. Both worked as grounds-keepers for the town golf course for the summer and helped Cassie out with transporting chairs, tables, dishes and food to their events. She definitely couldn't see either one of them as spies for the competition. Besides they would have no way of knowing who would call Cassie to ask for catering estimates for their events. So, for now, Cassie decided she had to let it go. Sighing, Cassie turned to the one thing that always helped soothe her worries – cooking.

Deep in thought while stirring the lobster bisque, Cassie barely heard the phone ring, but she definitely heard Jane answer it. No one could miss the bubbly, effervescent sound.

"Cassie's Cuisine. How may we help you? Mrs. Dinwoodie, wait…wait…hold on, I can't understand you. Please slow down. Mrs. Dinwoodie, are you all right? Oh, I see. Yes, yes, of course. What a shame. I hope…yes, of course. I believe so. What did you have in mind? And for how many? Okay. Could you hold a minute? Thank you."

Cassie stopped stirring the pot on the stove. "Let me guess, Mrs. Dinwoodie is in a dither."

"You guessed it. Apparently tomorrow is a big bridge tournament and it was supposed to be held at Mrs. Clausen's but this morning she was whisked away to the hospital in an ambulance."

"Oh dear, I hope it isn't serious."

"I have no idea. Mrs. Dinwoodie seems more upset by the fact that the event will probably now have to be held at her house. And she has nothing to feed this crowd of sixteen. She's talking about lobster sandwiches, crabmeat and you're supposed to suggest a couple from which she'll pick a third type." By now, Janie was getting worked up. "We're supposed to be getting ready for the Rodgers' wedding rehearsal dinner here tonight. And tomorrow we're catering the Wyman family reunion down in Harwich. How can we stop and prepare a spread for Mrs. Dinwoodie?"

Cassie walked over. "Let me speak to her." Taking the phone, Cassie put a smile on her face. Not hard, actually. She really liked the ditzy Mrs. Dinwoodie, a woman who was all heart. Putting her hand over the receiver, she asked Janie, "Is the conservatory booked for tomorrow afternoon? If Mrs. D. held it here, I'm sure we could manage."

"It's free, I remember looking over the bookings for this week-end."

Cassie turned to the phone. "Hi Claire, dear. How would you like to hold your bridge tournament right here in our air conditioned conservatory?"

"Oh, darling, that sounds absolutely marvelous. I have to call everyone any way to tell them we aren't meeting at Mrs. Clausen's house. That would be perfect."

"Now, have you thought that perhaps sandwiches could be a little messy for folks to eat? Might we serve some of our famous chicken stew, lobster bisque or clam chowder? Or for a change, the asparagus quiche is also a nice choice. They won't have to handle messy finger foods. And you could have some of our yummy rolls you're so fond of to go with them. What do you think?" Cassie kept her fingers crossed. Because they were her clients' favorites, she kept a good supply on hand at all times.

"I think the lobster bisque and clam chowder, yes. But I just remembered those absolutely divine sandwiches you make on the date nut bread. Remember?"

"Of course, the date nut and cream cheese. Do you need another choice to go with that?" Cassie asked.

"Well, we're having the seafood in the soup, so I wouldn't think a seafood choice. What else do you have?"

"There's always the chicken salad or hummus and tomato."

"No. I love both of those but they don't seem to fit. Perhaps I should just stick to the date nut."

"Here's another idea. We could vary the fillings. Include the cream cheese spread you like, but also we have a lovely apricot-orange cream cheese spread and another one is the carrot-pineapple-pecan spread. We can do them all on the date nut bread or have some on either the zucchini or pineapple breads."

"Ooh, that's it! Perfect," Mrs. Dinwoodie practically purred. Cassie swore Mrs. D got that sound from her long-haired kitty-cat, Mirabelle. She was a thin, cute as a button black cat with a white chest, and a tiny face with the longest fur Cassie had ever seen on a feline. And Mirabelle was more loving than many of the people Cassie ran across in her business. Of course, she was partial to cats. She looked over at Middy, now a senior kitty, who was curled up in a ball on her cushioned window seat. In the kitchen, Cassie had a bow window installed that overlooked the backyard just for Middy. She could nap in the sun or watch the birds at the feeders and birdbaths. Middy would chatter at the birds as they flew in and out of bushes and the maple trees. Strings of tiny white lights were strewn across the trees and bushes in the back yard. At night, any guests in the Conservatory could look out at the lovely display.

"Good choices," Cassie was telling Mrs. Dinwoodie. She often said that, even if she privately thought her clients were out of their minds with some of the oddball choices of food they chose to pair together. Occasionally she would try to steer her clients into something more appropriate but in this case Mrs. D's odd choice of sandwiches somehow fit her style perfectly. "Yes, and for dessert, either the chocolate cream pie," one of Mrs. D's personal favorites, "or the little cheesecakes topped with cherries?" Cassie was betting on the cheesecakes today.

"Oooh, the chocolate cream pie, of course. But what about that divinely delicious carrot cake you make?"

"Even though you're having the carrot cream cheese spread?"

"Oh, that doesn't matter, dear. I honestly don't care what the guests think of my choices. I'm simply going with what I feel like eating!"

Cassie wanted to shout, "Hurray for you!"

Finally the whole menu was planned. And Mrs. Dinwoodie had decided they better make it enough for twenty as she had several friends who had expressed an interest in joining the bridge club. She said this would be a perfect time for them to join.

"And how is grandmother, dear?" Mrs. D didn't seem to be in any hurry to get off the phone and actually, Cassie was enjoying their conversation. It kept her from thinking about the man that she was seeing everywhere she went. At the grocery store, she'd seen him at the end of an aisle, and at the Copper Kettle restaurant the other day, he was standing in the parking lot when she came out. After she saw him, he turned and swiftly walked down the street. By the time she got into her car and drove down the street, he had disappeared.

Is he stalking me? It certainly feels that way. The man seems young and has a thin build. He always appears in a Red Sox baseball cap with the brim pulled down his forehead, shielding his eyes from view. And a brillo-pad for a chin. It's some sort of beard. And the rate he chain-smokes, doesn't bode well for a long life ahead. Who is he? And what does he want with me? And should I tell anyone about this – yet?

"Cassie, dear?"

"Sorry, Claire. I was just wondering if your bridge club would be wanting snacks later in the afternoon."

"I should think just tea and coffee, dear. Oh, I would love to have those chocolate chip squares you make. Um, perhaps, yes – why not!"

Cassie nearly groaned thinking of all the rich food Mrs. D and her guests were going to consume. She didn't want anyone collapsing from clogged arteries on her watch. But, Claire Dinwoodie *loved* to eat. She was a short woman, generously built with a gargantuan bosom, but an even bigger heart. Cassie just hoped that Claire didn't eat too much rich food at home all the time.

After they confirmed the snack and financial arrangement, Cassie went back to answering Mrs. D's original question.

"You were asking about my grandmother. She

is so busy. As you know, she's involved in this Association of Cape Cod Volunteers that is sponsoring the Cook-Off. Of course, you know that, you're on their board too, aren't you."

"Indeed, but I tell you that Ginny, your grandmother, is probably our most active member."

"It's true, she really doesn't want to slow down. This girls' summer sports camp she organized is starting next week. I understand she has the girls' basketball coach on board to teach the girls on Monday and Tuesdays, 1-5 o'clock. Then she was trying to find a coach for softball for Wednesday and Thursdays. Last night she said someone was interested and Gram was going to meet the woman today."

"Oh, how splendid. That girls' sports camp is one of the things that our association is going to support with the proceeds from the cook-off. That brings the total to five organizations we're going to give funds to if this cook-off is successful."

"Let's hope so. I hear there are ten caterers who are going to set up on the field that day."

"Cassie's Cuisine is still one of them, I hope," Mrs. Dinwoodie asked.

"You bet. Gram would disown me if I didn't! Besides, we're all excited about participating and possibly winning the contract for the big fall fundraising dinner the Association is going to have in September."

Each caterer was paying the Volunteers' Association $50 to enter the Cook-Off. And although anyone could come to the event, they had to pay for any food they tried from the various caterers. Cassie expected a lot of children would be showing up so they were going to have hot dogs, chicken fingers and ice cream available plus one of her signature dishes – a seafood roll-up – chopped lobster, shrimp and scallops, ranch dressing, celery and paprika, topped with a little melted gruyere cheese. And they'd have a less expensive roll-up available to offer also – the hummus, tomato and onion. Cassie hadn't told this to anyone, even Jane. She didn't want Dorrie to find out.

Just then, Cassie felt Jane tugging on her sleeve.

"Oh, dear, I'm sorry Mrs. Dinwoodie, it seems I'm needed in the kitchen. Please let me know if we need to make any changes for tomorrow, otherwise we'll expect you just before 1:00."

"Bye, dear. Looking forward to it."

By the end of their discussion Mrs. Dinwoodie was practically singing she was so happy. Gone was the frantic voice of a few minutes earlier.

"What are you, some kind of granny-counselor these days, making little old ladies calm, cool and collected?" Jane asked.

"You know something, Janie, it's good therapy for me, too. I feel loads better than I did an hour ago."

"Well, now you're going to have to play marriage counselor. Mrs. Bettingill called. The bride's mother? It seems we have an even bigger problem. She said the bride and groom were fighting and they were threatening to call off the wedding."

"You're kidding? These kids are getting married Sunday and they're talking about calling it off?"

"Yup. She and the groom's mother, Mrs. Rodgers, don't know what to do about the rehearsal dinner tonight."

"Okay, I'll give Mrs. Bettingill a call. Tell the others to keep preparing the food. This wedding is not going to be canceled if I have anything to say about it. You mark my words, these kids are just letting the jitters get the better of them. Probably under so much stress from the families it's driving them up the wall. No wonder they're about to crack. We've seen it before, Janie."

Two kids. Ready to start the rest of their lives together. Twenty-somethings. Cassie laughed. She was only twenty-seven herself. But she felt old these days. So very old. And tired. Once again Cassie felt a wave of sadness threatening to pull her under. It was like this lately. One minute she was happy and a few minutes later she'd be blue. What was wrong with her? And let's not forget the times she's felt terror-stricken. Every time she's seen that wacko watching her. But that alternated with anger.

Let's face it, Cassie said to herself, "I'm an emotional wreck."

Some days it was hard to relate to the folks around her. Even her closest friend, Jane Jankowski, her assistant. Janie was only three years younger than Cassie, but frequently Cassie felt like they lived in totally different worlds. It was true of others, too, not just Janie.

Closing her blue eyes, Cassie let the weariness seep over her bones and fill her thoughts with gray shadows. Right now what Cassie wanted to do was to run upstairs to her room and close the door. Shut out the problems. Wouldn't that be giving in, though? *I've never given in to the despair. At least not yet. I have to find a way to keep going. But maybe it's time to do more than that. Time to break through this web of the past that keeps my soul churning and fighting through the shadows.*

Ten years ago when her best friend disappeared, Cassie's world exploded into tiny shards of pain-filled moments that never ended. Daily fresh assaults from Mrs. Avery added to Cassie's agony. Bobbie's mother alternated between accusing Cassie of helping Bobbie run away, to actually accusing Cassie of harming her daughter. And if Mrs. A wasn't doing that she was blaming Cassie for not doing more to find Bobbie.

It took every ounce of inner strength and every precious thread of faith she could cling to, for

Cassie not to dissolve into a complete breakdown. Many times she was close to slipping into darkness. A desperate bleakness always seemed a mere thought away.

That was then.

And now the night sweats were back. And the dark images that haunted her sleep had all come crawling back. Why? Why now after all this time? Was it the stalker? Or is it something much more sinister?

Cassie wondered if there was a person anywhere in the world who knew, really knew, how to heal old wounds. Was it even possible?

Sometimes Cassie turned the radio on and listened to music. Usually she could count on it to elevate her mood. But not today. Her favorite station was playing "oldies" from the Sixties. The last thing Cassie needed to hear was, *Eve of Destruction,*" the song that played when she and Jack were in Bobbie's bedroom searching for clues the day that Bobbie Avery disappeared from their lives forever.

CHAPTER TWO

Ginny Barton, Cassie's grandmother, had met with her new softball coach candidate. Vicki Doyle was perfect for the job. In Florida, where she came from, Vicki had coached the junior varsity softball team. She and her family had only just moved to the Cape. When Ginny got home, she immediately called Cassie's mother to come over for coffee. She had something very important to tell Shirley Wood, Cassie's Mom.

Cassie and Jane, Bonnie and Jessica, worked quickly getting everything ready for the wedding rehearsal dinner that would start at 6:30. Cassie had talked to the bride earlier. The young girl had just needed someone to listen to her concerns. She and her fiancee had been arguing so much recently that she had begun to question the wisdom of marrying him. This would be for the long haul. Were they really sure? Cassie had asked a few simple questions. *"When did you decide you wanted to marry him? And what about him made you think that you were right for each other?"* Questions like that got the bride thinking about all the great things that they loved about each other. Shortly she had wanted to hang up and call him and tell him how excited she was about their wedding and starting the rest of their lives together. All was well with the love birds.

Cassie looked at the clock, and she and the gang had only an hour and half left to get the food ready and the room set up. At that moment, Jessica and Bonnie were already in the Conservatory finishing up the place settings.

It was still light out so you couldn't get the full effect of the beautiful setting. The crystal chandelier hung above the banquet table. Although quite ornate and heavy-looking, the table was moveable on recessed rollers. The intricately carved "wooden legs" actually folded up, allowing for the table to be moved and the room to take on a different design and floor plan.

Soon the miniature white lights outdoors would come on, along with the chandelier, and change this place into a magical fairyland. At least that's how Bonnie saw it. She loved this room. In fact she was crazy about her job and the people she worked with. Well, most of them.

"I tell you, Bonnie, that Cassie is not the goody-two-shoes you seem to think she is. She's got you snowed, girl."

"Jessica, what are you talking about?" Bonnie asked, even though she didn't want to hear any more criticism coming from Jessica's mouth. She wished the girl had never taken this job. All she did was complain about the work and bitch about Cassie. What was with this girl?

"For one thing, do you think nice girls string along two boyfriends at the same time? That guy with the stupid name isn't the only one she's dating."

"His name is not stupid," Bonnie interrupted. "His name really is Ben Franklin, okay? And lots of women have men friends they do things with." *Don't they? she wondered.*

"Well, his parents were idiots then for naming him Ben. Anyway, she's seeing him at the same time she's been sneaking around with that pizza guy, or should I say, mobster?"

"Joe Picoli is not a mobster. And he owns a very successful Italian restaurant, not a pizza parlor."

"You're always trying to justify or excuse her. What are you, like teacher's pet?"

"Jessica, if you're so unhappy here, why don't you go work for Dorrie? She's a friend of yours, isn't she?"

"What are you talking about?" Jessica shouted.

"I've heard you talking with her on the phone. I bet Cassie would be interested in hearing that, don't you?"

Jessica, a big-boned gal that stood a half head taller than Bonnie, and weighed thirty pounds more than she did, towered over her co-worker.

In a hiss, Jessica threatened, "You tell her anything about me and you'll be very sorry. You don't know who you're dealing with. Believe, me you don't."

"What's that supposed to mean?"

"Just what I said. And I have no intention of quitting this job, so get used to it."

With that, Jessica turned around, planning on leaving for the day. But standing in the doorway in her way, was Cassie Wood, their employer. She had heard every word.

"Well, well. That explains who the spy is, doesn't it, Jessica. You are. And yes, you are finished. Pack up your things and leave. You are fired."

"You can't fire me," Jessica shot back.

"I just did. And you can tell Dorrie for me to stay away from my business and my clients. Tell her for me, there could be consequences. Think you can do that?"

"You will be so sorry, Cassie. Boy, will you ever." Fiery glints shot from Jessica's green eyes.

After Jessica stomped out, Bonnie said, "Oh, man. That is so wrong. I'm sorry, Cassie."

"You and me both, Bonnie. And now we're going to be one person short for this busy weekend – starting tonight."

"I don't know if you remember, but when you hired me I asked if you could use another gal and you said with me and Jessica you couldn't t take on another."

"That's right. I remember."

"My best friend, Sam, still hasn't found a summer job yet."

Cassie interrupted. "Sam?"

"Samantha Bishop."

"Do you think she'd be interested in starting work tonight by any chance?" Cassie asked desperately. "Not only do we have the wedding rehearsal dinner starting in about forty-five minutes, but we have to get ready for the Wyman family reunion tomorrow morning and then Mrs. Dinwoodie's bridge club at 1:00."

Bonnie called her friend, Sam, and in what seemed like a miracle to Cassie, the eager young lady said she'd be there in fifteen minutes, ready to work.

As Cassie was about to leave, Bonnie asked her, "I don't get it, Cassie. I mean we all know who our clients are, but how would Jessica know how much you've quoted on a new job?"

"The only way I can think of is that I leave folders of each job open on my desk. She had to have snooped."

Bonnie's face screwed up in an expression of extreme distaste.

Cassie left her to finish up the table preparations and hurried to the kitchen. "Janie, dear…"

"Ssh! Listen to this!" Janie pointed to the countertop television.

On the screen, the anchors for the early news were discussing the case of a young missing woman.

"Mary Chen was last seen at the Cape Cod Community College parking lot one week ago today. She arrived for her 8:30 a.m. class – a friend waved to her. But Mary never made it to class, as far as we know. No one in her class had seen her. Yet her car, a 1970 VW bug, was still in the lot. Police and volunteers combed the college grounds and many student volunteers assisted with searching the buildings. Mary Chen vanished without a trace. And there are no new leads.

"Folks are beginning to talk about the case from two years ago, the summer of 1974. A young girl walking her dog on Race Point beach in Provincetown found the brutally murdered body of a young woman. We call her the 'lady of the dunes.' She has never been identified nor has her killer been found. And then there's the case, seven years ago in 1969, when authorities found the bodies of four women buried in shallow graves in Truro. In 1970, Tony Costa was found guilty of killing three of the women. He was sentenced to life in prison at Walpole. While in prison, Costa wrote a novel he called, Resurrection. Although it has never been published, details have been released. Costa claimed a friend named Carl shot two of the women and both Carl and Tony buried the bodies in the Truro dunes. The other two gals he claimed died from drug overdoses and that Carl buried the bodies but Tony didn't know that until afterwards. Tony Costa committed suicide in his prison cell two years ago in 1974, just four years into his life sentence. And we are left with the question – Who is Carl? And where is he now? Even more importantly, Where is Mary Chen?"

A shiver crept along Cassie's spine, sending her body into a spasm of chills.

"Cassie, you're shivering. Are you all right?" Jane could see the little hairs on Cassie's bare arms standing straight out. The warmth of Jane's hand clasping her arm woke Cassie from her momentary freeze.

"Oh, darn, Cassie. I'm so sorry. I wasn't thinking. Of course you didn't want to hear about a missing girl."

"It's all right, really, I'm fine. I just feel so bad for that girl and her family. I know exactly what they are going through. A pain so deep – so sharp – that you almost wish it would finish you off. You find yourself holding your breath for minutes at a time until you start gasping and suddenly realize you're starving your body of oxygen and you weren't even aware. It's like that and more. Cassie sighed, a deep painful process and tried to let it all go.

At that moment, Ginny Barton and Shirley Wood came into the kitchen from Gram's apartment.

Ten years ago, Cassie Wood had struggled through the last six months of her senior year in high school. Her dreams of becoming an investigator had gone up in smoke. There was no way she could go off to college. She couldn't concentrate for five minutes at a time. The task of sitting in a classroom, listening to a professor expound on anything more complicated than a cereal commercial, was beyond Cassie's scope at the moment. Nothing sparked even the tiniest bit of interest. All she could think about was finding Bobbie. Days on end she drove around looking. She made phone calls. Cassie even followed a few people, tailing them for a day or so, hoping to find a clue, an answer, anything that might lead her to Bobbie. Cassie dropped twenty pounds before her grandmother finally intervened.

She talked Cassie into getting a job at a large and prominent catering business in Boston. It was perfect for her. Cassie loved to cook and she could follow directions for the most part. Eventually she became absorbed with her new work and learned the business from every angle. Four years later she decided she wanted a change of scenery and a catering business of her own. She'd met Jane Jankowski at the Boston company and they'd hit it off. Together, with Gram and their parents, the girls got together enough money to start a business. And Cassie raised the money to buy an old captain's home in Yarmouth on the Cape.

The bottom floor consisted of the Conservatory, the Hearth room, the huge, oversize kitchen, 24' x 34', that they'd had remodeled including a walk-in freezer. And then a small three-room apartment on the south side for Gram. Ginny had become a surrogate grandmother for Janie who didn't have any grandparents of her own.

Upstairs the large floor was divided in two. The south end, over her grandmother's apartment, belonged to Cassie – a bedroom and a huge den and bath. There was a back staircase that led to Gram's apartment. Janie had the same rooms at the other end of the house. The set up was perfect for all of them.

Out front over the long, covered front porch, hung the sign, "Cassie's Cuisine." The reason it wasn't named for them both, was that Cassie was the real owner and ran the business. Janie insisted. She liked being in the background and having Cassie in charge. Junior partner was exactly what she wanted to be and loved it. She'd never been happier in her life. And the name of the business was kind of cute.

"Cassie, honey, your mother and I need to talk with you," Gram was saying. "It's very important."

Cassie wiped her wet hands on a towel. "Sorry, Gram, it's a madhouse here. I fired Jessica and a new girl is about to arrive and so is the wedding party and families. Can't it wait til later?"

Shirley looked at her daughter. One of Cassie's eyebrows arched up to the right. That was a definite sign of Cassie's stress. "Of course, dear. We'll talk about it later."

"Hey, Mom, aren't you and Dad going to the Christopher Ryder house tonight?"

"That's tomorrow night." A huge smile broke out across Shirley's face. She and her husband had instituted "date" night once a week starting earlier in the month. It was working beautifully.

Gram and Shirley both pitched in immediately with the dinner preparations.

All seemed to be getting on track.

And then the phone rang.

"Cassie!" Ben shouted, when she picked it up.

"That...that woman is not going to be long for this world!" he shouted. "One of these days..."

"Now, Ben," she interrupted. "Don't say things you'll regret later. Can I presume you are speaking of Dorrie?"

"Of course. Who else could make my life this miserable?"

Ben Franklin owned and operated the Pastry Shop, a business he inherited from his folks. From the time he was a child, Ben had helped in the bakery, and not only was it his life but he absolutely loved it.

Cassie cringed. Dorrie had made more enemies than she had friends. Sooner or later her nefarious ways would catch up with her, Cassie was sure. And she reminded Ben of that, too.

"You know the Hernandez-Mathewson wedding next week that you are catering? I was asked to do the wedding cake, as you know. Mrs. Mathewson called me up today and said she was sorry, but that Dorrie had showed her a cake that she liked even better and the price wasn't quite as high as mine. Can you believe the gall of that woman?"

"Actually, I can, Ben. I got word a couple of days ago that the bride's parents were dropping us to go with Dorrie's Delectable Delights."

"What, why didn't you tell me? That...that snake! What are we going to do about this? She's stealing our business!"

"Calm down, Ben. I'm not sure there's anything we can do about it." And she proceeded to tell Ben about firing Jessica and how the girl had been feeding info to Dorrie.

He was livid on her behalf. Cassie had to calm him down again.

"You know who else is angry with her?" he asked. "Richard Price."

"How come?"

"You know that huge resort and conference

center he just finished building on Rt. 28? Well, last week he invited thirty of his biggest investors down for a lavish week-end – complimentary stays in the most expensive suites – being wined and dined and generally impressed with what their investment had created. Only problem was that the kitchen in his five-star restaurant wasn't quite finished so he hired Dorrie's outfit to cater the dinner. He had asked for baked lobster, caviar, you name it. Do you know what she served them? You won't believe it."

Cassie groaned.

"Chicken! She served these rich, fortune 500 guys baked chicken, mashed potatoes, canned peas and frozen broccoli. Can you believe it?"

"But, Ben, why would she do that? She had to know that it would upset Mr. Price in a really big way. I don't get it."

"Supposedly she told him that the lobsters were tiny and not baking material and she couldn't find any others. But that everyone loves baked chicken. He had already paid for lobsters and gotten chicken. So he says he's going to the newspaper to tell his tale and that he's going to sue her for fraud."

"Phew. She must have been crazy to pull that stunt. I still don't get why she did it. Anyway, she's soon going to have a whole passel of trouble. I can't see Richard Price letting this go, can you?" Cassie asked.

"Nope. You're right. Maybe I don't have to call and threaten her."

"Ben! Don't even say that in jest."

He wanted to go after Dorrie himself, but Cassie was right. The rational thing to do would be sit back and wait to see what the developer-millionaire, Richard Price would do to her. Maybe he'd bankrupt her or run her out of town. Either worked for Ben.

With that off his chest Ben's thoughts turned to Cassie. Ben pictured her sitting at her big, antique wooden desk. He remembered the day they'd found it at a flea market. She went crazy. Then, of course, came the hunt for the perfect chair. But it had to be just right, she wanted comfortable, not antique. So Ben could see her now sitting in her big leather chair, holding the phone next to her ear, her pixie light brown hair tousled and curly from cooking in the hot kitchen.

He could hardly get Cassie out of his thoughts lately, he was so in love. Ben embraced both sides of his girl – the light pixie-side that laughed with delight, and the somber Cassie who never got over the loss of her dear friend. He loved them both. And he wanted to tell her how very much she meant to him. But one thing worried him.

"Cassie, have you spoken to Joe yet?"

She settled back in her chair. Cassie had never meant to actually have two boyfriends at the same time. Ben had been a good friend to her ever since she moved to the Cape. But for a long time she didn't see him as anything but a friend. Then she met Joe Picoli and thought she fell madly in love. He was so interested in her, at least at first. Especially when he learned about Cassie's loss of her best friend. Joe offered to hire a private investigator to reopen the case. Even though she was touched by his caring, Cassie ended up getting confused, because Joe didn't want to hear anything about her work, her business, at all. That was puzzling. Plus, the more they dated each other, the more Cassie discovered they really didn't mix. Joe was a daredevil. He took so many risks and chances. And he always wanted to be on the go. One time he drove the two of them up to Sanford, Maine for the car racing. He loved it, she was bored silly. And by the time they got home to the Cape she was exhausted and had a flaming headache. In fact most dates with him ended that way – she wanted to sleep for days. And then one day out of the blue, Ben asked her to have lunch with him. That's when she finally realized that Joe and she weren't destined to be together. But Ben and Cassie liked many of the same things – long walks through the woods or on the beach. Hiking up mountain trails or sitting reading together. Or sightseeing and shopping. They read similar books and debated ideas together. But she hadn't found a way yet to tell Joe it was over. Until yesterday.

"Yes, Ben, I told him that I was sorry but I had entered into a committed relationship so I wouldn't be seeing him anymore."

"How did he take it?" Ben asked warily. He was one of the folks who questioned Joe's association with the Boston Italian mob. Ben suspected Joe's buying trips to Boston for food for his restaurant were much more than shopping trips.

"He was fine, Ben, really. He wished me well and he said whoever it is, is a lucky guy."

"Well, he's right about that. You know I'm crazy about you, don't you Cass?"

"Yes, well I'm pretty nuts about you too, Mr. Benjamin Franklin."

They made a date for Sunday night. They both wanted to see each other tomorrow night but Cassie knew with two events that day she'd be totally wiped out by night.

Cassie pictured him lying on his living room couch, a blue plaid velveteen material that felt yummy against your skin. Ben wasn't classically handsome, but his royal blue eyes twinkled and his smile was part mischievous and part mystery. It was an alluring combination. His rumpled blonde hair hung over his collar in back, and in front an errant blonde curl dripped down his forehead, flopping against his eyebrows. They both got on well with people, although Ben's temperament tended to be more jovial and humorous…well, except when it came to Dorrie St. John and Joe Picoli.

After they'd hung up, Cassie sat there a moment ruminating on yesterday's call to Joe. The tone of Joe's conversation wasn't a happy one. It surprised Cassie because she thought he must be bored with her. Maybe that didn't matter. Maybe people weren't supposed to say no to Joe Picoli. She didn't let on to Ben, but the hint of menace in Joe's voice actually did worry her a great deal. When he had uttered those words about "a lucky guy" his tone was totally sarcastic. But she couldn't bring herself to tell Ben any of that. He was worked up enough already about Dorrie.

There didn't seem to be anything Cassie could do about the "Joe" situation, although maybe she could talk to Jane later. That might not be a bad idea.

Then Samantha Bishop arrived, the new girl. Sam was a petite dynamo with a long braid down her back. From there, the evening took off with a running start. It began on a high note – Sam proved to be a fabulous worker and she caught on to everything fast. Not only that, the bride and groom had made up and the rehearsal dinner was a huge success. The groom's mother, Mrs. Rodgers, got up from the table during dessert and searched for Cassie. In the kitchen, she found Cassie, her grandmother and mother, Bonnie and Sam standing around eating chocolate mousse.

"Oh, sorry, Mrs. Rodgers," Cassie began.

"Please, all of you keep eating and enjoying yourselves. The dinner was excellent and I just wanted to thank you all for making this a lovely evening. Cassie, I wanted you to know I tried to talk the bride's mother into hiring your firm to cater the wedding Sunday but she had already booked Dorrie St. John's catering service. I really tried to talk her out of it especially after I got a call from Dorrie asking me to drop you from the rehearsal dinner and use her. She said she could tie a theme together with the wedding if she did both. I told her I was extremely happy with your business, having used your firm in the past. And that I didn't appreciate her trying to undermine other people's business like that."

Cassie couldn't help but smile. "What did she say to that?"

"Oh, she huffed and fumed and said she wasn't doing any such thing, blah, blah, and hung up." Mrs. Rodgers shrugged her elegant shoulders. She was dressed in an Yves St. Laurent original summer linen suit, not a knock-off. The Rodgers were a century's old Cape Cod family who earned their wealth through building homes across Cape Cod. They never flaunted it, but gave to numerous charities and volunteered for organizations just like regular folk. In fact, Mrs. Rodgers, Mrs.

Dinwoodie, and Cassie's grandmother were three of the five board members of the Cape Cod Volunteer Association that was running the upcoming Cape Cod Caterers' Cook-Off.

Janie, normally the "silent one," found the courage to speak up.

"Mrs. Rodgers, we want to thank you for giving Derek and Melissa Wyman our name. Their family reunion is tomorrow. Have you ever been to their cottage on Pleasant Lake?"

Chuckling, Mrs. Rodgers, asked, "Have you seen their cottage?"

In unison they all replied in the negative.

"Wait a moment," Mrs. R said as she went back to the room to get her handbag.

"Here we are," she said, returning quickly. Alma Rodgers pulled a snapshot from her wallet and handed it to Cassie. "As you can see, there are two couples in front of a house. They are Mr. Rodgers and myself standing beside Derek and Melissa Wyman. That is their so-called 'cottage' behind us."

Cassie's mouth dropped open. She passed the photo around. Judging by the astonished looks, everyone else was just as surprised to see a huge two storey house adorned with red-cedar channel siding. The windows on the lake side on the second floor ran from floor to ceiling, and Cassie suspected they were looking out from a cathedral ceilinged room.

"Wow! Like wow!" was all Sam said, and they all burst out laughing.

"By any chance has that house been shown in Architectural Digest?" Cassie's Mom asked.

"No," Alma said, "but it very well could be."

Cassie crossed her arms. "Does anyone else think that this house is wasted on a relatively small lake instead of being up the side of a majestic mountain somewhere?"

Janie nodded in agreement. "So this is where the reunion is taking place. Look at the side of the house – they have picnic tables in that clearing. I bet that's where we're supposed to put up our eight-foot tables and chairs tomorrow."

"That reminds me, we need to head over to the barn and make sure everything is on the truck except for the food."

Janie offered to come along. And then Bonnie and Sam chimed in, too. Gram and Shirley decided to stay put and chat with Alma a bit longer.

On Gram's side of the house was a long driveway leading up from the street all the way back to a very large barn that Cassie had made over into a laundry/storage area. A shorter circular drive ran off of it across the front of the house to a driveway on the opposite side. Cassie switched on the lights in the barn.

"Oh, look," Sam said. "What is that weird looking contraption?"

"That's an iron-pressing machine called a mangle," Cassie replied. "Although I've heard my mother use other, less-flattering terms for it."

Janie chuckled. "Believe me, it takes a lot for Cassie's Mom to lose her cool."

"If you aren't careful you can get quite a burn from it. We iron the tablecloths with it. It's a son-of-a-gun to operate," Cassie admitted.

Sam gulped. "Yikes. Will I have to learn to run it?" She asked, a bit scared.

Cassie put her hand around Sam's shoulder. "Oh no, not at all. My mother and grandmother take turns. They keep the linens up-to-date for us. Don't you worry, you won't have to go near the beast."

Peering in the back of the truck, Cassie saw the requisite number of chairs, tables and red oilskin tablecloths -per the Wyman's request. Thank goodness, Cassie thought. They are so much easier to wash and put away afterward.

The Wyman reunion was going to be a different type of affair than they usually did. The couple wanted them to provide all the food. Salads – potato, seafood and pasta; condiments; hot dogs and burgers ready to cook; veggies ready to be grilled; and scallop kabobs. They also required grills to cook them on. But Cassie didn't want to buy a second grill. They had one for outdoor events – a really nice, large gas grill. They'd be using it at the Cook-Off. She'd convinced Derek that where he'd probably be doing a lot of entertaining in his new beautiful home, that he might want to purchase such a valuable grill for himself. It worked.

The other strange part about the event was that Derek and Melissa didn't want Cassie and her people to stay. Mr. Wyman fancied himself to be a chef and wanted to do all the grilling and cooking himself. As long as everything, absolutely everything was provided, including drinks and desserts.

So, they had to drive all this stuff down to Harwich tomorrow and arrive well before 11 a.m. Of course, now Cassie and company would have to arrive earlier than planned in order to get back here and have the food and Conservatory ready for Mrs. Dinwoodie and her bridge group.

Back inside the kitchen, Shirley told the girls, Bonnie and Sam, to go home for the night and get lots of rest so they could be back here at eight in the morning.

"Janie, Cassie, up to bed, the two of you. Soak in a hot bubble bath and go to sleep for the next eight hours," Shirley said. "Your grandmother and I are going to clean up after the rehearsal party. Now shoo," she commanded, flapping her arms at them.

They were both too exhausted to argue. Wearily, the girls climbed the stairs to their floor. Normally at night they plunked down in Cassie's den for awhile, chatting about the day and about guys and other fun stuff.

"Cassie, I don't know about you, but I'm totally bushed. And I have a feeling tomorrow is going to be some kind of marathon." Janie yawned.

"More like a roller coaster, I'm afraid," Cassie agreed. "I think Sam is going to be a big help, though. She and Bonnie work great together. Much better than with Jessica."

"That's for sure. Now that Jessica's gone, do you really think that Dorrie will stop poaching our clients?"

"Well, she'll have a much harder time finding out who has hired us."

Janie yawned again. "Sorry, can't help it."

Cassie wrapped her friend in a hug. "G'night, Janie. Sleep tight." She put her arms on Janie's shoulders and turned her around, steering her down the corridor toward her bedroom. "Be sure to set your alarm – we better be up no later than seven!"

Janie sent a sleepy backward wave to her buddy as she slowly trudged to her door. She knew the minute she got to the bed she was going to fling herself down. Janie didn't think she even had the energy to change clothes.

Cassie watched until Janie disappeared inside her room. I hope I'm not working everyone too hard, she wondered, as she headed to her own room.

Finally, Cassie pulled the sheet up, and Middy snuggled up beside her in their queen-size bed. Even though it was a hot, humid night, it felt good having Middy snuggle close. Her purr helped Cassie unwind.

"Uh, oh, I forgot, Mom and Gram wanted to speak to me earlier about something. I'll have to remember to ask them about it tomorrow, Middy."

Settling in for a peaceful night of sleep, Cassie woke abruptly. Her breathing stopped. Barely lifting her head from the pillow, she peered toward the window. There was a noise. Middy poked her head up. That wasn't good. It made Cassie even more scared -- if Middy heard it, then it wasn't just a figment of her overactive, imaginative, terrifying nightmare. Or was Middy reacting to Cassie's fear.

She kept one eye on the window, the other one hidden behind the sheet. Cassie pulled it tighter over her face. Something moved in the window. *Oh, no, is the stalker there? Is that cigarette smoke I smell? Get a grip, Cass, you're two stories up. There's a tree. Would he climb it?* Sweat broke out across her chest. Cassie's heart pounded, jumping against her rib cage. Then she saw it. A twig from the tree branch scratched the window. Whoosh – Cassie's breath shot out from her over inflated lungs. Just a branch. A tiny one at that. *How can something that teeny reduce me to a tight knot of nerves and fear?*

That's it! She nearly screamed, getting out of bed. Cassie marched over to the window, looked out over the tree and yard and found no one lurking in the tree, the yard, the bushes, anywhere. She turned her back on the window and her fears. *I'm not going to be afraid any more. Next time I see that jerk I'm going to chase him down!* Middy blinked at her. *Aren't I?*

Saturday, June 30, 1976

CHAPTER THREE

The sun was up bright and early – way too early, Cassie groaned. And as they all soon discovered, the day grew hot and humid before nine a.m. which is when they arrived in Harwich at the 'cottage.'

Unpacking the truck and setting up for the lunch took over an hour. Cassie was grateful to see that the Wyman's had two huge refrigerators, allowing them to put all the perishables away. He wanted to know why they weren't putting all the stuff out now.

"Are you eating lunch in the next fifteen minutes?" Cassie asked, peering at her watch which read quarter past ten.

"No, of course not," he replied.

"Mr. Wyman you might not realize that food like this – potato salad, hamburgers, etc. can all turn bad very quickly if not kept refrigerated, especially in this heat."

He smacked himself up the side of the head. "Sorry, I wasn't thinking. Well, there are enough teenagers around here to help us bring it all out in a couple of hours." In fact most of the Wyman clan had arrived bright and early. Bonnie and Sam had counted sixty-two people so far, amazed that there could be so many folks in one family. Cassie made a mental note to ask them both more about their own families later.

They certainly had an idyllic spot here at the edge of Pleasant Lake. Cassie still felt the spot didn't warrant the huge mountain-retreat type of house they built, but it obviously made them happy. The smell of pine trees wafted on the air. While they worked, the girls saw a few motor boats and a there was boy trying to sail a sunfish. Unfortunately, there was hardly a breeze in the humid, heavy air. When was this weather going to break? Everyone would welcome rain. Well, maybe not in the middle of the Wyman's cook-out.

At one point when Janie was checking over the supplies they'd put out on the tables, she looked over across the lake and saw someone staring at them through binoculars. She dropped the ketchup bottle. Thank goodness it was plastic.

"Janie, what's wrong?"

Nothing gets by Cassie, Janie thought. In answer, she just pointed to the other shore. As Cassie gasped, her hand flew up to her heart. It seemed rather an extreme reaction, Janie thought, although, dropping a ketchup bottle isn't exactly a mild one, she reminded herself.

Sure enough, staring back at them through binoculars was a scruffy guy in a baseball cap -- Cassie was willing to bet it sported a Red Sox emblem – and there was that little beard, she thought, although it was hard to be sure at this distance – again with the brillo pad look – and the same stance as the guy who'd been stalking her. Cassie's late night bravado came back to haunt her. Did she really want to run over there and chase after this guy? There wasn't any kind of path. The Wyman's had a small sandy beach and a dock. But to the right of the beach tangled undergrowth had spread all the way to the edge of the lake. This whole end of the lake was inaccessible. The next "beach" area was where the stalker was standing, across the lake. To the left of the dock a small beach ran along the edge of the lake but that led all the way to the other end of it. Too far away.

Disturbed by Cassie's reaction, Janie bugged her.

"Cassie, WHO is that guy? And don't tell me he's a bird watcher."

Holding back the retort that she really wanted to give, *that she had no clue but was having nightmares about him,* instead Cassie tried to calm down and tell it straight.

"I honestly don't know who he is. I guess you could say he's been stalking me."

"WHAT?" Janie felt her insides quaking. She

had hold of a large knife and started waving it around in the air. This was serious stuff and Cassie was standing next to her talking like it was no big deal. She wanted to shake her out of her fantasy world.

"Two questions. One, why didn't you tell me and how long has this been going on? And two, why haven't you called the police?"

"Janie, I know math wasn't your strong suit, but that was three questions." Seeing that Janie was about to blow her top, Cassie continued. "Okay. By not talking about him, I guess I thought he'd eventually go away and I'd feel foolish. So I didn't tell you. Besides, I didn't want you to worry. And what would the police do, anyway? Doesn't the guy have a right to be wherever he wants if he isn't bothering anyone? And would you *please* put that knife down before one of us gets hurt?"

Hearing Janie and Cassie's voices carrying up from the beach, Bonnie thought she better check on them. She was sure neither of them realized they could be heard all over the place.

"Hey, you two. Voices carry out here."

"Oh shoot. Sorry," Janie apologized.

Seeing Cassie stare across the water, Bonnie looked over to see what was up.

"Hey, we've seen that guy before!" Bonnie shouted. "Remember, Cassie? At the grocery store the other day. He had that same weird jacket on.

See, he's turned around. The logo on the back is a hot rod with flames coming out the back."

Cassie staggered. The girls thought she turned her ankle on the uneven ground. Or even slipped on the pine needles that were strewn everywhere. They grabbed hold of her.

"Bonnie, are you sure of the hot rod patch on the back?" she asked.

"You bet. I got a good look when he turned around at the grocery store that day. Kind of strange, though, that he has the jacket on today in this heat."

Cassie looked across again, but he was gone. "It couldn't be," she whispered to herself. "Just a coincidence."

"What are you talking about?" Janie asked.

"Huh?" Cassie mumbled in a daze.

Janie wanted to go after the guy. "He was smoking a cigarette. There are signs everywhere that say don't smoke in the woods because of the bad drought we've been having. It hasn't rained in forty-seven days, did you know that? So he shouldn't be smoking out here. I want to confront him. I want to yell at him. I WANT TO FIND OUT WHY HE'S FOLLOWING YOU!" With her hands on her hips, and her tiny framed body, Janie looked like some kind of comic book hero. She just needed a cape, Cassie thought.

"But, Janie, what if it isn't him? What if it's not

the same guy that's been following me, but just some guy that looks like him?"

Janie mumbled, "Not likely."

Bonnie checked her watch and much as she wanted for them to have an explanation to all this, and put an end to this nasty situation, she knew that Cassie would be upset if she realized it was after eleven o'clock already. With summer traffic they'd be lucky to get back to Yarmouth in half an hour.

The girls had traveled separately from the guys in the truck. Now she had to round everybody up so they could all go back together. The Wyman's had generously offered to have them leave the truck in a spot away from their house but on their property. They'd need it later when it was time to come back and pack everything up. He'd said for them to return at seven o'clock tonight.

Cassie handed the keys of her station wagon to Kevin. He loved to drive and she just wanted to be quiet and think.

What did it mean? I've been seeing this guy almost everyday for the past week. Sometimes several times a day, different places. So far, the only place I haven't come across him is at home. Probably because our house is set way back from the road. We have the two long paved driveways that lead down to the clearing where the house is. Cassie's Cuisine, or as Janie and I like to call it, C & J's hide-out. At least our home hasn't been touched by this person. This stalker. Or is it? If Bonnie is sure about the emblem on the back of his jacket, that means it could be...no, how could it. Cassie sighed. *Let it go for now. There's work to be done.*

The six of them – Kevin and Tim, Bonnie and Sam, Jane and Cassie had piled into the station wagon. Sure enough, route six, the mid-cape, was basically a parking lot. It looked like a centipede from the overpass, and Kevin decided against taking the ramp onto the highway. Instead he got on the CB and learned from a trucker where he could pick up one of the back roads that would take them back to Yarmouth. It may have been winding roads, but at least they wouldn't sit and bake in a hot car, fuming about how late it was getting. He knew his cousin Cassie and how she strived to keep her clients happy. He really liked that about her.

The route did indeed prove to be less traveled and got them home quicker. As they pulled up, Cassie admired the purple irises and the pink rhododendrons in the front gardens and the long covered porch running the length of the house. She missed sitting back on the porch swings enjoying the evenings. Cassie, Gram, and Jane often did that in the spring and fall. Summer was too busy, and Cassie had to remind herself that it was a good thing.

If Cassie thought they were going to dive right in getting the luncheon ready, well, she hadn't counted on the little present waiting for them on the top step. The day was about to get a lot longer.

They all stood there, staring. Something was wrapped in newspaper, something lumpy. She wasn't sure she wanted to look. Cassie thought of herself as a modern woman, but she wasn't afraid to admit that there were times she wanted a guy to do some things for her. Like now.

Kevin sensed her fear. Her blue eyes widened in anxiety, and with her shoulders hunched, she looked on the verge of cowering. Wondering what on earth had his cousin so spooked, Kevin didn't think it was just a lump of newspaper causing her fear. He climbed the steps willingly and bent down to inspect the bundle.

Carefully pulling apart the newspaper, he jumped back, yelling, "Cripes." Instinctively, Kevin covered his nose. "It's a dead fish! What kind of sick game is someone playing here?" Kevin grabbed it up, intending to put it in the trash bin out back, but Janie told him to bury it in one of the fallow gardens. He didn't want the gals to see it. Someone had made an angry gesture by cutting off the head. Kev really didn't like the look of this at all.

"Cassie, is there anybody really, really mad at you right now?" he asked.

She almost laughed. "As far as I know, just one. Joe Picoli."

"Whoa!" Kevin and Janie yelled at the same time. Cassie looked at them both. That was funny. Not only that, their faces had turned a little red. Hmm, now that's interesting, she thought.

"I don't like the looks of this, Cass. It takes a twisted mind to do something like this," Kev said.

"Back up a minute. Cassie, what's this about Joe?" Janie asked.

Groaning, Cassie told her they'd have to discuss it later when they had more time.

"How do you know this isn't something to do with the stalker?" Janie persisted.

Now it was Kevin's turn to shout. "WHAT stalker?"

"All right, everybody, listen up." Cassie addressed them all. "Look, I wish we had time to figure this out and do something about it, but we can't right now. Believe it or not, we still have to get ready for Mrs. Dinwoodie and her gang of bridge-playing cronies."

A sudden, frightening thought struck Cassie like a blow.

"Gram!" She ran up the stairs and threw open the door. "Gram!" she shouted. It hit her that someone mean enough to leave the dead fish, could've done anything else they'd wanted. Did they get in the house? Is Gram okay? She went in search immediately.

The rest quickly followed her in. What greeted

them was a heck of a lot better than the foul package on the doorstep. The smell of warming lobster bisque, and a fresh-brewed pot of coffee greeted them in the kitchen.

"Oh Gram," Cassie said, wrapping her arms around her grandmother. "You are the absolute best." She couldn't help it, Cassie started crying, her head buried in her grandmother's shoulder. Was it stress? Was it some guy stalking her? Or ex-boyfriend who probably left a dead fish for her? Was it the strong emotions she was feeling for Ben? Or the opposite strong feelings she felt toward Dorrie St. John? Who knew. Maybe it was a stewed-up combination of everything and the tears were bound to flow sometime.

She cried a river. And Ginny just held her granddaughter close.

Janie wasn't surprised. She'd seen Cassie be strong so often and at times wondered what, if anything, would finally allow her to release all the emotions she'd been holding in lately. Janie scooted the others away to give Cassie and Gram some privacy.

After a bit, Gram steered Cassie toward her apartment and told Janie to keep everything moving. Glancing up at the kitty cat clock over the stove, Gram reminded Jane that Mrs. Dinwoodie would be arriving in about ten minutes. She asked that Jane let her know when she did.

Thanks to all the preparations that Gram had already done while they were gone, everything was in order when Janie answered the door.

Mrs. Dinwoodie grabbed her in a big hug. "Janie, dear, so good to see you. You look wonderful."

Janie thanked her and brought her into the Conservatory to see how they'd decorated it and set up the luncheon table. She explained that after they all had their lunch, the big table would be moved and individual bridge tables would be set up. Mrs. D was ecstatic. "It's perfect!" she squealed in delight. Her enthusiasm boosted Janie's spirits. She'd been pretty down, worried about Cassie. Mrs. D was better medicine than anything could have been. She was one of their favorite clients.

Mrs. Dinwoodie greeted her guests as they arrived and seated them according to some plan only she knew. Meanwhile Janie returned to the kitchen and found both Cassie and Gram busy at work. Cassie had poured everything out to her grandmother and Ginny had listened and promised they would all figure things out together. Cassie had felt much better and they both knew that they had to push it all aside for a time and get busy.

Janie went up to her best friend and grabbed her in a hug.

"Thanks, hon," Cassie responded. "I'm okay now. At least I think I am. How's it going in there?"

Janie told her how happy and excited Mrs. D appeared to be and she was loving playing the Queen Bee inviting her guests to her party. She's such fun to watch. Cassie decided to see for herself, but on the way, someone knocked at their front door. Of course it could be one of Mrs. Dinwoodie's group, not realizing that the entrance to the Conservatory was to the side of the house.

Only it wasn't one of Mrs. Dinwoodie's group standing on the threshold when Cassie opened the door. Not only did her mouth drop open, but Cassie felt light-headed, like she might faint.

"Hello, Cassie dear." And that's the last she remembered.

When she next opened her eyes, Gram and Janie were standing over her and Cassie found herself lying on the couch in her office.

"Thank goodness, you're all right, honey. Not only did you have a shock, but Janie tells me that except for a few nibbles here and there you haven't actually eaten a meal since breakfast early this morning," Gram said.

"I'll run and get some sandwiches," Janie offered. She hated to leave because she wanted to find out who the mysterious woman was that shocked Cassie so badly.

"Is she here, Gram?"

"Yes, your mother is talking with her in my little kitchen. And before you ask, don't worry, Sam and Bonnie are keeping Mrs. Dinwoodie very happy. Her guests are getting settled and the girls are bringing them the lobster bisque now. Everything is under control."

Cassie stared up at her grandmother. All of a sudden it felt like her world didn't make sense any more. She wanted to step away from it. Maybe she could figure it all out if she was an outsider looking in.

"No more questions until you eat," her grandmother ordered.

So that's what Cassie did. Gram left her in the office with Janie while the girls ate. And Gram went back to her apartment to see how things were getting along there.

After the girls had eaten a few of the little sandwiches, Janie couldn't stand it any more.

"I know you don't have to tell me, but I am absolutely ready to implode if I don't find out what is going on."

Cassie smiled at her good friend. She was sitting at her desk, sipping tea and eating yummy date nut sandwiches, and sitting in the chair beside her was her best friend and junior partner. Cassie thought her life was pretty darn good, even if it was getting a little weird. For some reason, with Janie here and the girls, too, she felt a beautiful sense of calm settle over her – a feeling she hadn't experienced in a long time. She knew she could draw strength from that to face the new, strange happenings coming her way.

"The woman that I was so shocked to find on my doorstep is Beatrice Avery, Bonnie's mother. I haven't seen that woman in nearly ten years."

"Oh – my – goodness!" With that, Janie found herself speechless. An absolute first. Neither one of them spoke for a few minutes.

"All I have is a whole bunch of questions," Cassie finally said. "Why has she looked me up?" Finishing up her tea, Cassie decided to go find out. She couldn't wait until later.

Janie agreed to check up on the bridge club and see how things were shaping up for their luncheon.

Walking across the kitchen floor toward Gram's apartment, Cassie paused, listening to the sounds coming down the corridor from the Conservatory – laughter ringing out, the clanging of silverware against china plates, the hum of voices, the rhythm of their lives playing aloud. They were happy sounds. Again, Cassie felt a moment of peace, or was it grace, come over her. Suddenly, she was startled from her reverie by something rubbing against her bare legs.

"Middy!" Her kitty was offering up her feline support. Cassie picked her up, not caring about the black hairs that would surely get all over her white polo top. They all wore the tops emblazoned on the pocket with "Cassie's Cuisine" in blue stitching.

And the other part of the "outfit" was some type of navy blue clothing – be it slacks, skirt, or shorts. Today, Cassie was wearing a denim wrap-around skirt. The kitchen smells calmed Cassie as well – the smell of heat coming from the cooling ovens, the aroma of freshly brewed coffee – a pot was always kept fresh and ready for everyone. Familiar smells and sounds.

"Okay, kitty-cat, I guess I've stalled long enough. Perhaps it really is time to try and lay the past to rest." She nuzzled Middy's fur with her nose and was rewarded with kitty kisses.

With a deep breath, Cassie knocked on the connecting door to Gram's place. *Let's see if I can get a little further this time before fainting. And remember, Cassie Wood, you are ten years older than when you last saw Mrs. Beatrice Avery. You're not a kid. That's good, keep up the pep talk. I own my own business. Oh Lord, what if she has bad news. I'm not sure I can take any more emotional mind-boggling news today.* Before her thoughts could get any worse, Gram opened the door.

Without a word, Cassie followed Gram into her small kitchen. Her mother, Shirley, sat in one of the chairs at the Formica table and Mrs. Avery sat in another. The remaining aluminum chair with the bright yellow vinyl seat must have been where Gram sat earlier.

Standing there in a daze, staring at the tableau,

it was as if Cassie was an audience member at a play – the actors sat at a table up on the theater stage, delivering their lines, playing their parts. She was watching, waiting for the right moment to applaud. That way this scene had nothing to do with reality. Nothing to do with her long missing best friend.

But when Beatrice Avery stopped talking and turned, Cassie couldn't help but blurt out, "Bobbie?"

"Oh, dear. I'm so sorry," Mrs. Avery replied, getting up from her chair. "How awful. And how thoughtless of me. I should've realized that when you saw me the first thing on your mind would be that I'd heard from Bobbie. I am so sorry, dear. No. There hasn't been any word in all these years."

"Uh, ladies," Shirley interrupted. "Excuse us, please. Gram and I need to discuss something and make a phone call. We will be right back. In the meantime, maybe you both can get caught up."

Mrs. Avery nodded. After they'd left, she turned to Cassie with her arms open wide. "May I, Cassie?"

In reply Cassie walked into her arms for a very warm, loving hug. The gesture totally surprised her.

"Why don't we sit down, Mrs. Avery."

"Please, Cassie, could you call me Bea?"

With her mouth open, Cassie asked, "Not Beatrice?"

"Oh no. Beatrice was a very unhappy, angry and quite miserable person. And after Bobbie went missing I became numb. Not just from valium, either. I felt bad for Jack. I wasn't much of a mother after that. Or a wife for that matter. But Bea has been learning how to live and to love over the past seven years."

Cassie got up and filled a mug with the fresh coffee Gram had on the counter. "Would you like some more, Mrs. Avery? Or, I mean, Bea?"

"Yes, I'll take some."

After they got the coffee straightened out and the cream and so forth, Cassie asked the first thing that came into her head.

"Seven years?"

Bea chuckled. "Yes, well, for two years I muddled through after Bobbie was gone. It was awful. I was barely there. Mentally or emotionally, that is. Physically, I hardly ever left the house. And my husband buried himself in his work. Absent all the time. Of course, I found out later that he had sought solace from his secretary, his pretty young thing. So the only sensible thing to do was get divorced." Bea paused, stirring the coffee. "You see, I fell out of love. With Dick, anyway. And Jack stayed away at college. After he graduated, Jack moved out to Hollywood to work in film. He's still there."

"Oh, that's cool. You can tell me about him

later," Cassie said, as she didn't want Bea to get side-tracked from her tale.

Bea laid down the spoon and took a few exploratory sips. Satisfied that it wasn't too hot, she had a big gulp. Courage, perhaps, to go on with her story.

"We sold the house and two months later Dick married his secretary. I moved into an apartment in Boston, of all places. Being in the middle of the city provided me with activity and new events. Things that didn't remind me constantly of Bobbie. It didn't really work, of course. I thought about her all the time."

Cassie saw the pain in her eyes. She reached over and closed her hand over Bea's.

A big smile came over the woman's face and she continued.

"I was at the Museum of Fine Arts one day – do you know I had never in my life been there? Amazing when you think I only lived about eight miles away from the city for twenty years. Anyway, I was admiring a particularly lovely Constable painting when this man came over to stand beside me. 'What does it make you think of?' he asked me. I turned and looked into the handsomest, warmest blue eyes I'd ever seen. And that was it for me. I wanted to spend the rest of my life with this man I didn't even know. Can you imagine?" Bea laughed.

Cassie shook her head. "How fantastic! I love

that story. Please keep going," she urged. "What happened next?"

"Are you sure you want to hear all this, Cassie?"

"Let's put it this way. I haven't had a lot of good news lately, so I'd love to hear about it!"

Cassie grabbed one of the chocolate chip bars that Gram had set on the table for them. While she chewed she listened raptly to Bea's continuing saga.

"So I told him that the scene in the painting looked like a place I wish I could visit."

"And? What did he say?"

"He said, 'Well, dear lady, then we should take a trip to England together some time. Would you like that? And by the way, my name is Brian Willows and I would be honored if you would accept my invitation to lunch today.'"

Cassie stared. "Wow."

"Exactly what I thought, too. Wow. And I couldn't get 'yes' out fast enough!"

"Let me guess. By any chance are you two married now?" Cassie asked.

Bea shook her head yes. "My name is Bea Willows and I hope someday you'll meet Brian. We've been married for seven great years. He owns a home in East Dennis – Sesuit Harbor, and we've lived there ever since we got married. And Brian is every bit as wonderful as I thought he'd be that first day we met."

A noise at the kitchen doorway interrupted them.

"Cassie, I'm so sorry to bother you," Janie said. "But Mrs. Dinwoodie wants to know if we have any soft instrumental music we can put on when they start their bridge tournament. I know we do, but I have no idea what to pick. You're so good at that."

"Janie, come in here a minute." When she joined them at the table, Cassie said, "Bea, I'd like you to meet my business partner and dear friend, Jane Jankowski."

"So pleased to meet you, dear," Bea said, standing and shaking her hand. "I wish you had time to join us, but I understand how busy you both are. Cassie, thank you so much for taking the time to listen to me. I know that you will both be in the Cape Cod Caterer's Cook-Off and I knew that I'd be seeing you there. I just didn't want it to come as too much of a shock. You see, our mutual friend, Alma Rodgers, has just recruited me to join the Volunteer's Association."

"Wonderful. I look forward to seeing you there. And I really would love for us to get together and talk again. Do you think that would be possible?" Cassie asked.

"Of course. I'll look forward to it."

Bea and Cassie hugged. Gram must have been nearby as she walked into the kitchen just as Cassie and Jane were leaving to get back to work.

As the girls were walking to the Conservatory, Janie asked her if she was okay. With a genuine smile on her face, Cassie stopped and turned to her. "Yes. Yes, I really am okay. I'm not sure why, but maybe to think that something good happened for Bobbie's mother, makes things a little bit better. That doesn't make any sense. Bobbie is still missing. I can't explain it, Janie. But I'll tell you all about it later on when we can finally sit down and relax."

Janie laughed. "Sit down? Relax? When is that – September?"

Still chuckling, Cassie walked into the storage room off the Conservatory. In there they stored china, silverware, napkins along with tablecloths of all sizes, six folding card tables, extra folding chairs, crystal goblets, and also a dual sound system so that music could be piped into either the Conservatory or Hearth Room or both. Cassie grabbed the ninety-minute cassette she wanted and plunked it into the machine. Turning on the power and pressing the start button, Cassie expected to hear the opening bars of Mozart's piano concerto in C. Instead, she got, "Big Girls Don't Cry...y...y.." by the Four Seasons. "Whoops! Wrong golden oldies." She heard laughter coming from the Conservatory. Sticking her head out, she heard clapping. Cassie went in to see what the big attraction was. Only she forgot to stop the tape. All these senior bridge players, currently still munching on dessert were having a ball singing to the lyrics.

Mrs. Dinwoodie motioned her over to the table.

"I'm so sorry Claire, I picked up the wrong tape by mistake. I have two "golden oldies" tapes. One is of the Sixties, which is playing, and the one I meant to pick up is called Mozart's golden oldies."

Claire laughed. "Honey this is perfect to finish up our luncheon. Isn't it everyone!"

They all clapped again. Cassie shook her head. You just never know about folks and what they'll like.

"Maybe once the tournament starts we better have the other one," Claire suggested.

"Absolutely. Does anyone need anything? Please don't hesitate to ask."

A dapper older gent stood up and it took a moment to recognize Ben's father, Thomas Franklin. Cassie was so excited she ran around the table to give him a big hug. She loved Ben's parents.

"See, aren't you guys jealous," Tom said to the three other men at the table. The bridge club consisted of twelve women and four men and today four newcomers had joined them.

Cassie's face turned red. And she had no idea what to say.

"This talented young lady is dating my son, Ben, and I'm happy to tell you that he's head over heels for this gal. My wife and I are nuts about her too. And isn't she a fabulous cook?"

Everyone at the table stood up and clapped, which just made Cassie's face turn even redder.

"Now that I've thoroughly embarrassed you, Cassie, dear, I tell you this was the most scrumptious luncheon I've attended in a very long time. On behalf of all my bridge-mates, we thank you." And he gave a gentlemanly bow.

Cassie tried to think of something but the only thing that came to mind was, "Who is ready for more coffee and tea?"

Bonnie and Sam had been standing unobtrusively in the corner waiting to see if they could help with something. Both had been enjoying the praise heaped on their boss. She deserved every bit of it and more, Bonnie thought to herself.

Someone else was thinking a few thoughts about Cassie. Tom Franklin thought his future daughter-in-law, as he thought of her, looked too thin, too wan and completely fatigued. He vowed to speak with her before he left. Some vitamins, some iron and a lot of rest is what he'd prescribe if he was a doctor. But he was just a retired baker, one whose regimen included health food, vitamins, exercise and rest. He was a perfect specimen of the healthy lifestyle – trim and fit, full of energy and life.

Except for the bullet wound in his leg. Four years ago at a conference in Boston, Tom was innocently walking by a bank at the wrong time. Bank robbers came barreling out of the bank waving guns. Tom was collateral damage with a shot to his leg. Unfortunately it shattered a bone and Tom now walked with a limp. One good thing that came out of that horror, was that he met Special Agent Sean O'Hara. They'd remained friends after the investigation and the trial. Tom Franklin missed playing golf, but he found plenty else to do.

Cassie put Bonnie in charge of switching the tapes when the group was ready to settle down to play. That way Cassie, herself, couldn't screw it up again. What had Cassie been thinking about?

It was Dorrie. There were flashing red lights going off in her mind each time she thought of Dorrie.

Ever since Ben told me that Dorrie pulled that awful stunt with the chicken dinner, I've been worried. I remember when I first came to the Cape I visited several of the local caterers and Dorrie St. John's was one of them. We hit it off right away. Dorrie is a little older, probably in her thirties, but she was vibrant and happy all the time. Then about a year later she completely changed. For the last four years Dorrie has been trying to undercut everyone, she growls and hangs up if I try to call and talk with her. This huge type of change doesn't happen for no good reason. I should've tried to find out a long time ago what went wrong for her. It's hard to believe that people can change that drastically. It was Dorrie in the beginning who told Cassie that the catering world, at least here on the Cape, was about helping each other out whenever one of us needed it. I can remember Dorrie calling one day asking me to share a job that she'd just gotten. We put the event on together. Something that would never happen today, that's for sure.

The feeling of unease was so great that Cassie decided she had to do something about it. She waited until they changed the "luncheon Conservatory" into the "bridge tournament Conservatory" before going to her office to make a call. She couldn't ignore the feeling any longer.

At the other end of the line an unfamiliar voice answered, "Dorrie's Delectable Delights. How may we help you?"

Clearing her throat Carrie answered, "May I please speak with Dorrie St. John? Tell her it's Cassie Wood."

"Well, I'm not sure Ms. St. John is taking any calls," the voice on the other end said, suddenly turning snippety.

Cassie sighed. "Please just ask for me," she responded in her quietest, most reasonable voice.

"Fine, hang on," came the ungracious reply.

Several minutes later, Cassie heard someone pick up the phone, then a squeaking noise, as if someone settled into a chair.

"Hi, Cassie," came the dullest inflection of voice Cassie could imagine coming from Dorrie.

"Hey, how are you? I've been thinking about you a lot, Dor."

"I can't imagine why."

Again with the monotone. That really puzzled Cassie. Dorrie was either fierce or hissing, that seemed to be her range lately. But this? What was this?

"I was remembering when I first came to the Cape and how you helped me out so much. We really seemed to hit it off. And I've been ashamed to say that I didn't keep in touch and haven't tried to see how you've been doing."

Dorrie was quiet. "Why would you want to do that? What do you care?"

For a second, Cassie pulled the receiver away from her ear and stared at it. Not that the receiver itself could solve this enigmatic situation, but Cassie was simply baffled. Might as well ask her outright.

"Dorrie, are you okay? I'm concerned."

Cassie heard thumping, as if Dorrie was nervously bouncing a pencil on the desk.

"Yeah, well, I guess you could say things aren't going so hot. Listen, you can't tell anyone this stuff, okay?"

"You have my word," Cassie responded sincerely.

"The business hasn't been doing so good and neither have I. For a long time now I've been getting headaches, but lately they've been worse. So much worse. I've had to step back from the business a bit. Well, maybe a lot. And I don't like what I've been finding out has been going on around here. Plus, I take the pills the doctor gave me, but they don't help. And before you ask, no it's not a migraine."

"Wow. This is a lot, Dorrie. Especially about your health." This sounded serious. "Has the doctor done a cat scan of your skull?"

"Huh? What do you mean?"

"Probably nothing, but I should think he'd want to rule out if there is some bruise or something in there. Know what I mean?"

"Gee, I don't know, Cassie. You sure it'd be worth the money to find out nothing is wrong? I mean, then what?"

"Well, that's a good point. But I guess if it were me, I'd want to make them keep trying until they got to the bottom of it. I'm willing to bet you haven't felt like yourself for a couple years, have you."

Dorrie snorted. "Now, how would you know that? Got spies, have you?"

"No Dorrie, I track it back to when you first started changing. Going from the happy, carefree gal that you had always been, to this unhappy, angry person that you seemed to morph into."

Dorrie wanted to answer angrily. But either she didn't have the energy or deep down she knew Cassie was right.

"Well, I guess it wouldn't hurt to see the doctor again."

"In the meantime, Dorrie, if you need help with something, all you have to do is ask me, okay? I mean it." Cassie had wanted to find out more about the business, like what on earth happened at Rick Price's investors' dinner, but Dorrie's health was much more important.

Cassie didn't know it, but tears had formed in Dorrie's eyes, and as they began to drip down her face, she wasn't sure she could utter another word. Cassie's kindness helped more than anything had in a long time. With it came a resolve to get to the bottom of whatever was going on in her head. Dorrie picked up the phone again and called her doctor.

Before they'd said good-bye, the gals made a date to have lunch with each other after Wednesday when the 4th was over. That day– the day of the great COOK-OFF, loomed large in everyone's mind.

As soon as they were off the phone, Cassie wanted to talk to Ben right away about Dorrie. She had a suspicion that they'd all been viewing this whole Dorrie affair from the wrong angle. Perhaps what she needed was people rallying around her, not jumping all over her.

"The Pastry Shop."

"Hey Ben. I've been talking with Dorrie and it's looking like what's really been going on is that she might be sick. I think she's going to need some help."

Ben looked at the phone and wondered what universe Cassie was coming from now. "Why on earth would I want to help that woman who has caused nothing but misery for all of us."

"Because she really might be ill, Ben. She's had awful pains in her head and they're going to be doing a cat scan of her skull. It may partly explain why she's acted the way she has."

"Really? Do you believe in the Easter bunny, too?" he asked.

"C'mon Ben. Try and give her the benefit of the doubt. She really could be sick."

"Yeah, and it could be that she's just a mean, vindictive..."

"Ben!"

"Witch, ok? Mean, vindictive witch. What if she isn't sick? Then what?"

Cassie thought a minute. "She's had financial problems with the business. I don't know. I just know that when I first came to the Cape, Dorrie reached out to me and helped me. We became good friends. Then I guess I got busy and kind of let our friendship slip away. Now I just want to see what's going on. I really think something has happened that has made her change so much. If I can help, I want to. You can understand, can't you?"

"Sweetheart, you are one of the kindest, most understanding people I know. Cass, you're amazing."

"Aw, Ben, not really. But does this mean you'll help?"

"Sure okay, why not. By the way, is there something in the coffee you guys drink over there? The whole bunch of you are all sunshine – or, I know – you guys dine on too much of Gram's chocolate cake, the sugar high turns you all nice."

They talked for a time about the Cook-Off. Cassie had decided against serving ice cream. Logistically it probably would have been too difficult. Even though all the caterers had pitched in together to rent a refrigerated truck for the afternoon, it still seemed like too much to handle. Besides, Ben told her the Volunteers' Association had hired an ice cream truck for the event. So Ben had offered to make desserts for Cassie's Cuisine to sell at their stand. Ben, not strictly being a caterer, but a baker, didn't have a booth in the Cook-Off. Cassie thought his idea was fabulous and they discussed the goodies they'd have for sale. Ben was excited to be helping them out that day.

After that, Cassie did paperwork at her desk

until Janie popped in. Cassie had no idea that an hour had passed.

"Hey, Cass, aren't the bridge-playing wizards supposed to be getting some afternoon snacks?"

"Oh my goodness, I totally forgot. The chocolate chip squares, remember?" Cassie flew out of her chair and they hit high gear pulling together the "snack."

Finally, the bridge players were happily satiated and were down to the last two tables of players left in the tournament.

Cassie checked the kitty cat clock over the stove and it read four o'clock. They'd made it through this long day -- so far at least. The girls, heaving a collective sigh of relief, each grabbed a cup of coffee from the never-ending pot and plopped down onto their favorite kitchen stools.

Janie hated to burst everyone's bubble, but reminded them, "In a couple hours we have to be back down to Harwich to pick up the stuff at the Wyman's."

A collective groan reverberated through the kitchen.

"But wasn't that house just absolutely awesome, or what?" Sam gushed, thinking back to the 'cottage.'

"Yeah, it wasn't too shabby," Janie agreed.

Bonnie worried about what had happened down there and wondered why no one was talking about it. And let's not forget the dead fish!

"Cassie, do you have any idea who that guy with the binoculars is?" Bonnie asked timidly.

Cassie thought a minute, not really sure if she should air her suspicions or wait. Well, wait for what? She asked herself.

"Look, guys, I don't actually know who it is. But Bonnie, if you are right about the emblem on the back of the leather jacket – a hot rod with flames coming out of it, then there's a tiny, slight possibility it could be someone from my past. But very doubtful."

"Here." Bonnie pulled a sheet of paper out of her pocket. Her hobby was drawing and she drew two pictures. On one side of the paper was a rendition of the 'stalker' and the other side showed a better picture of the hot rod and flames.

"Wow, this is great, Bonnie," Cassie replied. "I had no idea you had this fantastic talent. Seriously, you are so good."

Bonnie blushed. "Thanks."

Taking another look at the pictures, Cassie was now almost sure it was him. Back then he didn't have the brillo pad beard. Other than that, she was looking at a picture of Lenny Marek.

She told the girls the story of Lenny and Bobbie. And then of her last moments with Bobbie and how they'd fought over Lenny. Cassie thought back. He had graduated with the class but then, like many others, Cassie never saw him again. Until now?

"I don't know what it means. Why he's here, if it's him. Why he's stalking me. Now? If he blamed me for Bobbie disappearing he could've come to me a long time ago. Why now? I'm sure he wouldn't hurt me, though. Lenny made himself out to be a tough guy, but he never really did much of anything wrong."

"Maybe this guy is actually harmless," Sam said. "I mean, he didn't make any threatening moves. He hasn't said anything to you, has he?"

"No, that's true," Cassie replied.

A loud bang made them all jump. Except for Bonnie. She had slammed her hand down on the counter.

"No threatening moves?" she yelled. "What do you call that dead fish wrapped in newspaper that lay on the doormat when we arrived back this morning?"

Cassie hadn't forgotten about that. But she hated having to explain what she really thought happened. If Janie didn't like the stalker, she was really going to hate this.

Heaving a huge sigh, she began. "It probably wasn't from him."

Waiting, Janie put down her coffee cup. She knew Cassie and she had a funny feeling about whatever Cassie was about to say.

"I don't know for sure, but I kind of think it was from Joe."

Janie stared at her and Sam asked, "Who is Joe? We have two maniacs after you?"

Cassie laughed. The others soon joined in.

"What?" Sam asked. "What's so funny?"

"Perhaps just the absurdity of it all, Sam. How many people can say they possibly have two deranged individuals after them at the same time?"

"Eeew," Sam replied. "Not good, buds, not good at all. But Cassie, we've got your back. Don't we guys!"

"Here, here!" they all shouted raising their coffee cups in the air, clinking them together like a toast. At the last second, Cassie joined hers to theirs. "Thanks you guys."

"So, now explain Joe," Janie demanded.

"Dear sweet hyper-active Joe didn't take our break-up too well. And as much as I've pooh-poohed the idea of him having mob connections I think I've come around to that conclusion finally. After all, a dead fish sounds just like something a mobster might do, don't you think?"

Three heads bobbed in unison.

"Awesome. Two bad guys," Sam said out loud.

"Crikey," Janie shouted. "I've never heard of someone having so much drama in their life as you do right now."

Cassie's mouth squeezed together and Janie

regretted her outburst immediately.

"I take it back," she said. "The drama is ours – and we're all going to fix it together. Right gang?"

They converged on Cassie, embracing her in a group hug.

I'm so lucky, Cassie thought. Even more than that, I feel very blessed to have such wonderful friends. I'm surrounded with folks who love and support me. It sure doesn't get much better than that.

Breaking up the love fest, Cassie announced she better check on Claire and her group. It was awfully quiet down the hall.

"They're probably at a crucial spot in the tournament. Better just watch a few minutes so you don't break some champion's concentration," Jamie warned.

"Good idea – don't want to upset the customers."

Cassie got up and was just starting toward the hall when someone knocked at the front door.

"No! Oh, no! I AM NOT ANSWERING THAT DOOR!" she shouted.

Janie laughed. "Hold onto your britches, girl. I'll get it."

Janie opened the door to a very distraught woman whom Cassie thought she recognized, but couldn't come up with a name. She knew she'd met her before, but her brain was a little fogged at the moment.

"Cassie! I have to see my mother right away!"

That's it, Cassie thought. Mrs. Dinwoodie's daughter…what's her name… Helen.

"Helen, what's wrong?"

"It's my daughter, Gigi. I…she… it can't be…."

"Do you want to sit down?" Cassie asked, concerned that Helen might faint just like she had earlier.

"No, I have to get my mother. Oh, my girl. My Gigi… She's missing!"

Monday, July 2, 1976

CHAPTER FOUR

The rest of Saturday had been somber and heart-wrenching. Cassie and Jane had sent Claire home with her daughter, Helen, and had given them tubs of clam chowder and sandwiches with explicit instructions and a promise that they would eat something later. Helen looked to be on the verge of collapse, but the girls knew that Claire would rise to the task of getting Helen and her husband, Steve, through this horrific ordeal. The woman possessed amazing strength. Claire and her husband, may he rest in peace, as Claire often said, both lived through the Depression and the second world war. She would survive this and help others to do so. It was her nature and we are all blessed because of it, Cassie thought.

That evening a very quiet group had ridden to Harwich to pick up after the reunion. All of them volunteered to stay late to unpack the truck, wash everything down and put stuff away.

It seemed that this summer, which Cassie had to remind herself, had only just begun, was off to a very long and difficult start. At the end of the season, would she and Jane look back and ask what all the fuss had been about? Perhaps that would have been true, except that now there were two missing young women. They needed to be found. With every fiber of her soul, Cassie prayed they would be found alive and well. And soon.

Yesterday was Sunday and Cassie had planned to do some cooking. They had an event to cater on Monday and she needed to get some things ready ahead of time. Her plan was to have Janie take the day off and spend it with Kevin. It was obvious they were smitten with each other. Then in the afternoon Cassie had hoped to spend it with Ben. Instead, after what had happened, with Gigi missing, she and Jane got up at six a.m. and cooked until eight-thirty. The four of them joined the volunteer group that the police were assembling to search for Gigi – Georgina Shepherd. Bonnie and Samantha also joined the search.

~~~~~~~~~~~~~~~

Saturday around one p.m. Gigi and her girlfriend went to the Cape Cod mall in Hyannis. They were going to a swimming party on Sunday and had each wanted to get new bathing suits, so off they went to Filene's. Once they were inside the building, Gigi had announced that it was freezing in there and she would run out to the car to get her sweatshirt. Her girlfriend, Sara, waited for her to return. And waited. After fifteen minutes, Sara grew concerned. They had been lucky. A parking spot had opened up close to the store so Gigi should've been back in ten minutes, tops. But, of course, Sara thought, Gigi probably ran into someone she knew in the parking lot. Smiling then, Sara later told police, she was sure Gigi was held up talking with some friends.

"Gigi is one of the most outgoing, caring people I know," Sara had told them.

Sara was just down the hall from the door and would've seen Gigi come back in. When she didn't, Sara had hiked back down to the entrance where she could see the car and see who Gigi was gabbing with. But the car was there – and Gigi wasn't! That's when panic started. Gigi couldn't have missed which entrance they'd come in, because it was practically right next to their car. Sara had then run out to the parking lot, checked in the car, and found that Gigi's sweatshirt was gone. So she had been there. But then what happened? If she had come back into the mall, Sara definitely would have seen her. Sara had looked all around the parking lot, thinking Gigi might have walked over to a friend's car. It was eerie, Sara had told the police, and she had felt completely alone and desperate. She decided to search around on the pavement, hoping maybe Gigi had dropped something that would give

Sara a clue as to what happened. But all Sara saw was some old cigarettes and gum. Gigi was now missing twenty minutes and Sara felt herself going into panic mode. Droplets of sweat formed on her chest, yet Sara had started shivering. "I knew something was horribly wrong," she had told the police.

Numb with fear, Sara remembered running back inside. She wanted to scream. Where was the security office? She spied a security guard and from there it all began.

There was no sign of Gigi anywhere.

~~~~~~~~~~~~~~~~

Sunday the search that Cassie and the group joined was conducted all over the grounds at the mall and surrounding areas. And inside the building, every single nook and corner. Cassie and Ben, Kevin and Jane were part of the group searching Filene's. The girls went in every single dressing room and bathroom. They searched the whole store from top to bottom. Nothing. It was as if Gigi simply vanished. For hours volunteers came and went. There were fifty stores in the mall, the biggest ones being Filene's, then Sears and Woolworth's. They debated sending teams to search every single store but in the end the authorities asked the store managers to have their employees search inside their stores for Gigi. Then police brought in tracking dogs. But the trail, starting at Gigi's car, started and stopped there. It went nowhere. After an exhaustive search, the police finally concluded that Gigi had been abducted right there by her car.

~~~~~~~~~~~~~~~~~

So Monday found a very sad group gathered at Cassie's. They were doing their best to pull the luncheon together to take over to the Institute – The Southeastern Regional Institute of Psychiatry, Psychology, and Research, known to the workers as PP&R. Cassie almost hadn't taken the job as it's only two days before the big Cook-Off, but at this stage it was best not to turn down business if she could help it. Finally they were ready and left.

The building was over in Brewster. The drive was a quiet, dreary ride. It didn't help that the weather had finally delivered on its stormy promise. Rain fell lightly as they finally pulled up in front of the three story, old brick building. On arrival, Janie exclaimed, "This place gives me the willies." She shivered.

Cassie couldn't blame her. Even with lights shining from inside, the building was a cold desolate place. The surroundings were deserted. Back a hundred feet from the building stood a thick forest.

Kevin drove the car up to the front entrance so they could find out where to unload and park the car.

At the front desk they all had to stop and get badges as no one was allowed to simply walk in and wander around the place. The security guard directed them to a side entrance that would take them closer to the kitchen and cafeteria where the luncheon was being held. Apparently once a year the Board of Directors singled out certain members of the staff for awards or bonuses based on their record during the year. For some unknown reason, this year the Board had decided to hire someone to cater the affair.

They unpacked the food in the rain.

"This place is spooky," Kevin said as he was lugging in cartons of food and supplies. "It looks like a setting for a horror movie. What on earth do they do here?"

Cassie had asked that herself when she was trying to decide whether to take the job. It was explained to her that they had some live-in patients but plenty of outpatients as well. They came for counseling, testing, and some took part in research and clinical trials. Counseling could be done with their therapists, but some needed further care and saw the psychiatrist who could prescribe medicine if it was needed. Cassie didn't like the sound of any of it, but neither she nor Janie had actually heard anything bad about the place, so here they all were.

Cassie would have loved to explore, but she was a little bit afraid. It was probably best to ignore everything but getting the food ready and onto the tables. It was being served buffet style. There were three eight foot tables set across the side of the cafeteria, closest to the kitchen. On these, the gang set out the foods. One table held cold foods, another hot, and the third was where folks could get their tea and coffee. Dessert would be served directly to the people from trays that the servers would take around.

"There you are, Miss Wood." A thin, but rugged man in about his thirties came up to her.

"I'm Dr. Jameson, Director of the Institute. How nice to meet you in person," he said, offering his hand. "I expect everything to go off like clockwork. I will shortly tell the employees to come up and get their food. At precisely one thirty I shall begin the award ceremony and you will hold off on dessert until I give you the signal to bring it out. Are we clear on this?"

"Yes, Dr. Jameson. I'm sure it will be fine."

"Good, good. I sincerely hope so. You have come highly recommended so I expect this to work. Alma Rodgers speaks well of you and your outfit. I look forward to sampling your work. Now, excuse me, I have to get back. Good day."

"Good day, Dr. Jameson," Cassie said to his retreating back.

Janie flung down the towel she'd been wiping her hands with. "What an officious, pompous…."

"Hold that thought," Cassie interrupted. "You never know who is lurking nearby. We best be careful. All of us. Clear everyone?"

"What's he mean, 'sampling our work?'" Sam asked. "Isn't the guy going to eat the food?"

"Hey, listen up," Cassie headed off any comments. "I'm serious here. Yes, the good doctor is used to directing events around him. Let's give the man an event so great he'll be forced to rave about us. We all on the same page now?"

"Yes, boss," Janie answered while the others nodded their heads.

Cassie knew that Janie only used that term when she thought Cassie was being too bossy, but Cass had a feeling that this event had the makings of being quite good or going really downhill. She wanted them to do everything they could to make it run smoothly. She had an ominous feeling, but wasn't sure where it was coming from.

As they finished putting the food out, the guests were arriving, taking their seats. Up at the head table an attractive brunette took the seat to the left of Dr. Jameson.

Bonnie happened to see her and exclaimed, "I know her! That's Kat Puskas."

"Excuse me?" Janie asked. "What kind of name is that?"

"Hungarian," Bonnie answered. "Puska literally means gun. Kata and her husband, Laslo, escaped from Hungary twenty years ago in 1956, during the Hungarian Revolt. It was a scary time."

"Okay," Janie said. "So how on earth do you know her?"

"Well, see, I'm taking Psychology at a night course. It's the adult continuing education courses. And Kata is the teacher. She's terrific, I love it."

Cassie walked over to her. "That's great, Bonnie. But I'm curious why you picked psychology."

"It's really fascinating stuff. I'm enjoying it so much. And that's partly thanks to Kat,...um...Dr. Puskas."

For the next half hour they were incredibly busy, dishing out the food. After endlessly listening to Dr. Jameson drone on about the Institute and its goals and eventually give out his five awards, Cassie and the others finally got his signal when he said, "And now without further ado, we can all relax with coffee and dessert."

When Bonnie was delivering the dessert choices to the head table – "Black Forest trifle or strawberry shortcake?" – Kata surreptitiously slipped a piece of paper into Bonnie's pocket.

When she got back to the kitchen, out of sight of the folks in the cafeteria, especially far away from Dr. Jameson, Bonnie opened the note and read it.

"Cassie, listen to this. It's from Kat. She says, 'I need to speak with you. Please don't leave until I have an opportunity. Will try to during dessert. Kata.'"

"Wow, high intrigue," Janie responded.

Cassie thought it sounded rather mysterious and hoped Dr. Puskas wasn't going to drag Bonnie into anything.

Working together, they served the forty-six guests their dessert choices. Some of the men had wanted to try both. As usual, Cassie had brought an abundance of everything to make sure everyone was happy.

About ten minutes later, as the party was starting to break up, Kata Puskas walked into the kitchen. She first checked to make sure that the Director was involved in a conversation with someone else and not looking this way.

Cassie moved over next to Bonnie so she could hear whatever the woman had in mind. She was feeling quite protective of her young protege.

Kata first praised the luncheon. "Such excellent food. I thank you very much. Truly delicious – and that Black Forest trifle was absolutely scrumptious – decadent, really with the chocolate and cherries."

Seeing her tongue licking her lips made Cassie smile.

"Dr. Puskas, you are quite welcome to take some home for dessert with your husband for later," Cassie offered.

"You are very kind." Kata snuck a look out the door. "Sorry, I must keep an eye out for his highness."

The others chuckled. Bonnie asked, "Are you referring to Dr. Jameson?"

"Most certainly, my dear. But please don't tell him I said that."

Bonnie said, "My lips are sealed."

"Here, I'll watch for you," Kevin offered, moving over to the kitchen door to guard the entrance.

"Why thank you, young man."

Cassie introduced the rest of her group to her.

After the niceties, Dr. Pukas quickly launched into her problem.

"The reason I wanted to speak with all of you is I was hoping to figure out a way to get an investigation started. I tried on my own and didn't get anywhere."

"What?" Cassie exclaimed.

"Our assistant director, Dr. Virgil Mennin, has been missing since the seventh of June. He simply didn't show up for work one day. And that led to the next day and so forth. As far as we can tell, myself and other members of the Board, no one has seen or heard from Dr. Mennin since June 7th. When some of us questioned Dr. Jameson about it, he insisted that the doctor had simply taken a leave of absence. It's quite absurd. Virgil's assistant came to me the day after he didn't show up. Christine said they were in the middle of conducting a research experiment with some students, and that Virgil would never leave in the middle of his own experiments. And she's right. I may not like the man. In fact, I've never cared for him, there is something quite shifty about Virgil. But even so, it isn't right that he's missing and no one is doing anything about it." Dr. Puskas sighed. "I wish that was all. This past Thursday, what is it, four days ago? Christine didn't show up for work. This got me worried. So I drove to her house. Her car is in the driveway. I asked her roommate about it and she's scared witless. She claims that Christine believes that Dr. Jameson and Dr. Mennin are doing secret experiments or research somewhere else and that is where Virgil is. She went to the police but they say there is nothing they can do. No one has actually reported him missing. The next day, right after Christine talked to the police, she vanished. You're not going to believe this next part. I asked Dr. Jameson what he thought happened to her. Know what he said? She went on a vacation. Well, that's news to her roommate and to her own mother. And apparently she went without taking her pocketbook or anything else with her."

"Holy cow!" Sam shouted.

"Exactly, dear. Excuse me, Jane is it? I'm sorry but does that coffee urn next to you still have any octane left?"

"Absolutely, Doctor. I was just about to pour a round for all of us. I'd be happy to make this first cup yours."

Kat relaxed her shoulders. She could tell, just standing with these young people that they were a caring bunch and maybe she would find a little help among them.

"I was wondering," Cassie began, "has Christine's mother talked with Director Jameson?"

"Good question. I had encouraged her to do so. And apparently when she followed through, he was unavailable. That was Friday. Today she called me and told me that when he wouldn't take her call, she went down to the police herself. At that point Christine hadn't been missing for forty-eight hours so they couldn't do anything. So Saturday she went down again. But, of course, that's the day the other girl, Georgina Shepherd, went missing. So the police were quite involved with that. They said they knew for a fact that Georgina had been abducted, and they still felt there was nothing to prove to them that Christine wasn't off on her own somewhere. That's why I've come to you folks. I have no idea where to turn next."

"Unbelievable," Janie mumbled. "Idiots."

"Okay, kiddo," Cassie stopped her before Janie could go off on one of her rants. Dr. Puskas,…"

"Please call me Kat," the doctor interrupted Cassie.

"Okay, Kat. I have a friend who knows a special agent in the F.B.I."

"Wow. Who's that, Cassie?" Bonnie asked.

"Remember the bridge group we had Saturday?"

"Oh right. Was he the handsome one who sang your praises?" Bonnie teased.

"Yeah, yeah. Anyway, Tom knows Special Agent Sean O'Hara out of the Boston office. I think we can talk to Tom and ask him if he thinks Sean would be interested in this case."

"That sounds like an excellent idea," Kat said. "Seems like the F.B.I. should be involved anyway, now that we have these two abductions."

Janie spoke up. "Three, remember? Mary Chen went missing last week at the college."

"She's right," Cassie added. "I bet the F.B.I. will be very interested, at the least we have kidnapings, but hopefully nothing worse."

"Battleship on the horizon!" Kevin shouted. "Man your stations, ladies."

"Huh?" Kat asked.

Cassie interpreted, "That's Kevin's way of saying your Dr. Jameson is headed our way."

"Dr. Puskas, are you in there?" he shouted from the doorway.

Kat continued sipping her coffee. In a normal voice, she answered, "I'm in here, William, if you care to join us."

He stomped into the kitchen. "What are you doing in here?"

"Excuse me?" Kat replied.

"You know what I mean."

"I'm afraid I don't," she smiled sweetly while replying. "I congratulated our chef on an excellent luncheon."

The Director crossed his arms. "I hope that's all you've been talking about."

"As a matter of fact, it isn't." Kat couldn't help but hesitate a minute, waiting to see his reaction. "I was reminding Bonnie, here, that tomorrow evening's class is canceled as it is the night before the 4th. I do wonder though, William, why it is that with your colleague missing, you aren't more concerned. What is going on that you don't want the authorities to become involved in finding him? Or Christine, either? It is curious. And frankly, it is damaging to you."

"Dr. Puskas, you see some of your patients here at the Institute, don't you? That privilege can easily be revoked, you know."

"Oh please, William. You call that a threat? You forget that in Hungary I was hunted down by men with machine guns, fired upon, and forced to flee for my life. Your puny threats are more tiresome than anything. But while we're at it. Much of your funding comes from the government. If an investigation of your practice was opened, I imagine that would be quite disastrous for you."

Dr. Jameson marched up to her, putting his face inches from hers. "I would be very careful, Kata. I believe you have a daughter just a little younger than some of these girls that have disappeared. It would be such a shame if she joined them, don't you think?"

Kata's face went white.

What on earth was going on, that he would make such a serious, horrific threat? Cassie wondered.

On hearing it, Kevin, Cassie, Janie, Sam, and Bonnie converged on Jameson, surrounding him. Cassie got up in *his* face.

"We don't take kindly to having our friends or their families threatened. Only the worst kind of scum does such a thing. And now we have you, Dr. Jameson."

"What are you talking about. You don't have anything. You're nobodies. Who do you think would take your word over that of a respected doctor? That's laughable."

"Play it, Janie."

Janie rewound the cassette. They always had their portable cassette player with them, as they played music softly while they worked in the kitchen. When he had walked in, Cassie nodded to Janie to start recording.

"Listen to this, mister," Janie snarled. And she

played back his words. His frightening threat to Kat's daughter stood out in all its menace.

"As I said, Dr. Jameson, we have you. If anything happens to Kat or anyone in her family, I guarantee you will spend the rest of your miserable life in prison. Am I clear?" Cassie asked, in a very quiet voice, strength coming through word.

"You aren't prepared to tangle with me, missie. All of you, be afraid."

With that ridiculous threat, he left.

Looking around at her shocked crew, Cassie noticed someone missing.

"Hey guys, where's Tim?" Cassie asked, concern in her voice.

"Don't worry, Cass. He left awhile ago to find the men's room."

But Cassie did worry. She wondered whether to send Kevin out to find him, when Tim ran through the back door.

"Sorry if I worried you, Boss. Let me catch my breath."

Kat headed over to the coffee pot and wished it was something stronger. She was still completely shaken by Jameson's threat of her daughter.

"After I heard Dr. Puskas' story about the missing assistant, I decided it would be a good time to go snooping. The Director was obviously busy talking with everyone so I went in search of his office."

Cassie's mouth fell open. She was flabbergasted. "Are you serious? What if you'd gotten caught?"

"Well, one of the security guards almost found me, but I hid under the desk when he came in. Listen, I've got stuff to tell you."

"All right, hold it. I seriously think we need to get out of here," Cassie announced. "When we get safely back at headquarters we can hear Tim's news and figure out our next steps. Kat, would you like to join us?"

"I would love to, but I'm going home first to check on my family, then I'll meet you there, okay?"

"Of course. Oh, is there a phone around here? I need to make a phone call before we leave," Cassie said.

"Yes, there is a payphone in the cafeteria, but why don't you follow me to the office. I share space with another psychologist, but she's probably not there right now. That will give you more privacy."

"Janie, while I'm gone, can you get everyone busy finishing up here so we can leave as soon as possible?"

Janie clapped her hands. "You heard her, kids. Let's get this show on the road." After they loaded the dishwashers and started them up, and lugged their supplies out to the car, Cassie came back. They all climbed into the station wagon and took off in a hurry.

On the way back to the house everyone talked at once. Cassie tried to make order from the chaos but everyone was upset. Plus she imagined they were all cranky because no one had stopped to eat lunch while they were at the Institute. Something she would remedy as soon as they got home and unpacked.

CHAPTER FIVE

The rain continued to fall, heavy at times, across parts of the Cape. In Yarmouth, the fog came rolling in from the ocean. The skies threatened to open up any moment.

He looked out the window and couldn't see to the end of the parking lot. At this moment he would rather have been out in a boat in the fog. His chances would be better than they are now. And he especially wished he had never picked up the phone. Hanging up wasn't an option.

The voice on the other end was saying, "I'm very disappointed in you. You were supposed to deliver the package by now. Your deadline has come and gone."

He was too scared to answer.

"So, do you have the package yet?"

'Uh, no.'

"Lost your connection, have you?"

"Only temporarily, Louie."

"What did you call me?"

"Sorry, Mr. Balboni. Look, I have other avenues I'm following." He paced back and forth, back and forth on his office rug.

"You're running out of time. Your continued success, on so many levels," continued the gravelly smoke-filled voice, "if you get my drift, hinges on your finding that package for me. That was the deal."

"I will, Mr. Balboni. I will. A little more time is all I need," he stammered, clearing his throat.

Mr. B was silent so long, he thought he was going to have a heart attack if the guy didn't speak.

"Friday, my friend. Just so you know – today is Monday."

"Um, couldn't we make it next Monday – you know – give me a week?" he gulped.

"Are you crazy?"

Certifiably, he thought to himself.

"You *must* be crazy – I give an order – you follow, get it? You don't get to make changes – you don't get to make suggestions – and you don't get to have ideas of your own. You get to follow instructions, period. Or maybe you need a little demonstration?"

"No, no, Mr. Balboni. Got it. Absolutely – Friday."

The boss hung up – slamming down the phone.

"Ouch," he said, the sound ringing in his ear.

He flung himself down in his chair and ran his fingers through his black hair. He sat there tapping his fingers on the desktop. "Friday? There's no way. That's it. I'm a dead man!"

~~~~~~~~~~~~~~~~~

At least there were no dishes to unload from the car. They had used the ones at the cafeteria and then put them through the two dishwashers there. They made it home just as the rain started coming down in torrents, so now they had to lug in the containers of extra food and the heat warming pans. Bonnie and Sam volunteered to stay in the barn, cleaning the stuff and putting it away. Of course, the fellows offered to stay and help them. Janie glanced backward at Kevin, probably wishing he'd follow her into the house. But Cassie was sure he was just doing his share of the work.

"Don't worry, he's not sweet on Bonnie or Sam. It seems that Kevin is pretty crazy about you. Even I can see that," Cassie told her.

"Are you sure?"

"Positive. Now can we pick up the pace and get in out of the rain?" Cassie complained. The girls started running and both of them hoped they weren't going to drop the containers of leftover food.

"Wow, that smells terrific," Janie exclaimed when they'd reached the kitchen.

"Yummy, Gram," Cassie agreed. "What have you got on the stove?"

"It's chili with a touch of curry. There's salsa and chips laid out in the Conservatory. I know you gals and I'm pretty certain you haven't eaten lunch." She shook her head. "All that food in front of you and none of you geniuses think to eat a thing. Amazing."

Cassie told Gram about the whole affair – about the missing psychologist and his missing assistant, Christine, and the police not believing she had vanished or been abducted. They foolishly believed the 'vacation' story put out by Dr. Jameson. And Janie told her about Dr. Kata Puskas and finally the threat by Dr. Jameson against Kat's daughter.

Gram had been incensed with anger toward the man.

"It's unspeakable, it's criminal for him to get away with saying such a horrible thing. Who is this man that thinks he's so untouchable?" Gram asked.

Cassie agreed with her. And truthfully, she was afraid for Kat and her family. Maybe they should suggest the family take a vacation – a real one – until this was resolved.

Jane, Cassie and Gram went into the Conservatory to start their lunch. Half way through, the doorbell rang. Cassie had called Ben and his father from the Institute and it might be them arriving. Or Kat. Janie answered the door and came back with all three of them.

"Ben!" Cassie shouted, getting up and running across the floor into his arms. "Wow, you cannot imagine how happy I am to see you."

"Same here, Cass," he said, still hugging her, and lightly kissing her cheek.

While Cassie introduced Kat to Ben and Tom Franklin, Jane and Gram left to get more food – Gram had made a chocolate cake that morning. Kat said she was still full from the fabulous lunch, but Ben and Tom dug into the chocolate cake with gusto.

Just as they were about to discuss the situation, the four kids from the barn came strolling in. Gram handed them bowls of chili. Kevin came over and scooted a chair in next to Jane. Cassie was happy to see a smile light up Janie's face.

Finally, Tom told them that he'd reached Agent O'Hara and given him the whole story, starting with the missing Mary Chen and ending with the absent Dr. Mennin and Christine's disappearance. He also included Director Jameson's threat to Kat and her daughter.

Cassie looked over at Kat and crossed her fingers. "Don't keep us in suspense, Tom," Cassie said.

"Sorry, but this coffee is delicious. By any chance, did you make it, Mrs. Barton?"

Gram flushed. "Why, yes, Thomas. Thank you."

Ben couldn't believe his father was flirting with Cassie's grandmother. "Dad!"

"Oh, hold on, son. Anyway, Sean was extremely interested in all of it. He told me he had to pass this up the ladder to see what red tape they had to go through to investigate the case. Usually, Sean said, they can't just swoop in and take over a local investigation, even if there are federal issues involved, like kidnaping. He's going to call me back later on. If he gets the go ahead today, Sean said he'll pack in a hurry and start down to the Cape right away. With any luck he'll be here at least by tomorrow."

"What a relief," Kat said. "Finally someone is going to take this whole thing seriously. Do you think there's any chance that this whole thing is related?"

"Well, Christine's disappearance, unfortunately, could be either of two things. One, the same person who abducted Mary Chen and Claire Dinwoodie's granddaughter, Gigi, might have taken Christine. Or, maybe something strange is going on at the Institute – could she have found out something she shouldn't have and her disappearance is linked to that. Although that does sound a little extreme." Tom finished.

"It's not unreasonable to think that Dr. Jameson is up to something. I've felt that way for awhile and some of the Board members agree with me. We just haven't been able to figure out what's going on," Kat said. "I don't know how we can find that out."

"Oh no, Kat, don't even think about investigating on your own. You have to protect your family," Cassie said. "Besides, Tom here will vouch for Agent O'Hara, that he's excellent at his job."

"That's a fact," Tom assured Kat.

They all sat quiet a moment. Finally, Ben said the one thing that probably had been on everyone's mind – even if just for a moment.

"Where are they all?" he asked. "Are they alive? Or heaven forbid, already dead."

Complete silence reigned in the Conservatory. Cassie looked outside and saw the rain slashing through the tree branches. The storm raged outside, not helping the gray mood that seemed to envelope the small group. Normally, they would soon be switching on the outside miniature lights. Even on the nights they had no events scheduled, Cassie and Janie loved watching them. Especially when the lights bounced on the branches in the wind. For a minute she wondered what the weather forecast would be for Wednesday, when they had the big Cook-Off and all the fourth of July celebrations. But her thoughts soon returned to the sad reality of the missing girls. There *had* to be something they could do. Then she remembered something.

She looked over and saw that Tim and Kevin had finally finished eating. Tim was deep in conversation with Bonnie, and they were laughing softly. Bonnie viewed herself as a plain girl, not one the boys paid attention to, even though both Cassie and Jane had told her on numerous occasions how pretty and bright she was, and how any guy would be lucky to spend time with her. Bonnie was short and quite thin, but a very sturdy gal, very athletic. She wore her hair in a Dorothy Hamill cut. In fact, Dorothy was one of her heroes. The skater had just won the gold medal at the Olympics this past winter. Cassie didn't know if this was a phase Bonnie was going through, but Cassie knew her young friend had a heart of gold. They made a cute couple, Bonnie and Tim, but he better not break her heart, Cassie thought to herself.

She hated to interrupt them, but Cassie felt they had to keep this meeting going and Tim might possess an important part of the puzzle.

"Say Tim, you never did tell us what you found out in Director Jameson's office."

Ben looked at her. "Cassie, what are you talking about?" She had to explain to him how Tim had sneaked up to the director's office when he wasn't there.

"Cripes, I forgot," Tim said, his red bangs falling over his face. "I was just about to give up, because I hadn't found anything interesting anywhere when I decided to look under his desk blotter." Tim smiled big. "I found a folder. It wasn't marked, but inside it was a letter from some government agency. I scanned it, and boy did I wish I'd had a copy machine handy. The letter was a rejection from the government for funding for some experiment that Jameson wanted funds to conduct. I was kind of afraid by this time that I'd been there a long time and sure enough that's when I heard the guard coming down the hall. I grabbed the folder and hid under the desk." Tim could still feel his heart pounding a jungle rhythm, fast and loud. "After he left, I finished trying to read it. The gist seemed to be that Jameson had an idea for an experiment about fear and drugs. I think he was trying to say that between a certain drug that he'd invented and fear-coping techniques, that it would keep soldiers from developing something called post-dramatic stress syndrome or something like that. He said take away the fear in the first place and they'd be better soldiers and they wouldn't come back with that syndrome thing."

"So why did the government say they didn't want to fund it?" Ben's father asked.

"I believe the person said there was no way to conduct such an experiment in a humane way. The things soldiers see and experience in war are so horrific, that you couldn't reproduce that to test the drug and the techniques. It was along those lines, I believe. Oh, and they said fear can also be a healthy thing for a soldier. It can keep him alive. If he doesn't feel fear, he might try to engage an enemy unwisely and get himself killed. I think it went something like that."

Cassie turned to Kat. "Did the Board at the Institute know anything about this research or this new drug?"

"Sort of. William was excited about this drug he co-invented along with a friend, a scientist with a background in biology and chemistry. They said they had the drug ready for the clinical trial stage. And were waiting to hear back from the government with the go-ahead."

Janie asked, "Is this letter Tim saw, a rejection of the trials, do you think?"

"No, not at all. It sounds like William wants to do a different kind of experiment, not really a clinical trial. I don't know if this was to be in addition to the trials, or what."

The group talked on for awhile but it was clear there was nothing they could accomplish right now. And the consensus seemed to be that what they really wanted to concentrate on was helping Sean and his upcoming investigation into the missing girls – Mary Chen, Georgina "Gigi" Shepherd, and Christine, who they learned from Kat had the last name, White.

Finally, everyone had left and Cassie was alone with Ben.

"You know what I think, Cassie?"

She shook her head.

"I think we need to get you out of here. Let's go do something different."

"What, like go for a hike in the rain?" she asked, sarcastically.

Ignoring her tired jab, he said, "We're either going out for a nice dinner, anywhere but Joe's restaurant, or we're going to my place and order pizza, stay in, watch movies, and throw popcorn at each other and have fun."

Cassie actually brightened up. "I vote for that one."

CHAPTER SIX

Tuesday morning Cassie woke up refreshed. She was ecstatic that she'd had no nightmares, no imaginary visits from her stalker or anyone else. Just pure sleep.

Last night Ben had driven her home a little after one a.m. When they came up the driveway, Cassie saw the house looming large against the gray, moonless night. A lacy pattern of spider webs with tiny, clinging raindrops lay across the evergreen bush by the porch stairs. The intense rain had passed but the air was still heavy with moisture. The porch light vaguely glowed in the misty fog and the dripping air. The only other light on in the house shone from Gram's rooms. She was surprised her grandmother was still up.

Cassie had been very glad that Ben had driven her home and that she hadn't had to walk up to the house alone. They were surrounded by a creepy atmosphere of shadows and wind.

Once inside, Cassie had gone to Gram's rooms and chatted a bit before heading upstairs to bed. Checking on Janie, she found her friend fast asleep.

Back down the hall to her own room, Cassie had climbed into bed with Middy, and slept that dreamless sleep that she had missed so much lately. A perfect beginning for the day, Cassie thought.

And by ten a.m. Tuesday, when there had been no dead fish, no stalker, and no reports of more missing girls, Cassie and Janie both remarked what a wonderful day it was turning out to be. Even the bad weather had passed and the sun peaked out from behind some clouds.

The girls were busy checking supplies, making lists of food and things they still needed for the Cook-Off tomorrow.

~~~~~~~~~~~~~~~

Ginny Barton, Cassie's grandmother, was stymied. She still hadn't found the right opportunity to speak to Cassie about something very important. Trying a different approach, Ginny decided she had to take things into her own hands. To that end, she had invited Vicky Doyle, her new softball coach for her girls' sports camp, over to her place.

At first Vicky was reluctant to come. But Ginny held her ground and told Vicky it was time. Sooner or later Vicky was going to have to take care of this situation and Gram thought that it had to be today.

Around ten a.m. Vicky arrived and walked up to the side door of Gram's place. She hung her head.

Vicky knew this day would come eventually, but she didn't believe she would ever be up to the task. She came up with quite a number of excuses as to why this should be put off. When she got inside, she tried out a few of them on Gram, but Ginny Barton knew something about life. She guessed you didn't get to be her age without learning a few of life's lessons along the way.

"Enough, Vicky. Deceit is a corrosive force. If you don't clear this up now, it will wear on you. And besides, you can be certain this will come out one way or another. Time for you to own up to it and take care of it."

Vicky groaned and shook her head, her short brown hair bouncing from side to side. Tears appeared to be forming in her blue-grey eyes, but Gram wasn't about to give in now.

She said to her, "I'm getting Cassie now and you better be here when we get back or I'll tell her myself, and things will only get worse."

While Gram walked away, Vicky wiped her eyes. Her misery was part sadness and part fear.

The girls were in the walk-in refrigerator discussing mayonnaise, celery and chick peas among other things when Gram walked into the big kitchen.

"Cass, honey, I'm sorry to bother you, but I really need you to come over to my place for a few minutes."

Janie and Cassie were both dressed in blue cotton slacks and their white cotton polo tops and they were both freezing.

"Sure, Gram, anything to get warmer. Have you got hot coffee going over there?"

"Sure do. Just finished making a fresh pot."

"Gee, can I come too?" Janie asked. "Just kidding, Gram. I've got plenty to do, believe me. And besides, I think I'll get our own coffee pot going. I have a feeling we're going to need it."

Cassie followed her grandmother and wondered what was going on. Nothing – nothing in the world could've prepared her for what happened.

When they got inside the apartment, Gram stopped.

"Honey, I have no idea how to tell you this. None whatsoever."

And just then Vicky Doyle came out of the kitchen and Cassie's heart stopped. Her mouth dried up, her stomach lurched and she became nauseous. Cassie thought she was having a heart attack.

"Bobbie?" she screamed.

Vicky stood still, but her insides shivered and played ping-pong.

"Hi Cassie. My name is Vicky now."

Cassie's eyebrows scrunched together, her forehead wrinkled, her mind couldn't wrap itself around seeing this girl, this woman now, who ten years ago had been her best friend. Someone Cassie imagined had probably been killed long ago. Yet she was here. Right here. Alive. And apparently well.

"Where the hell have you been?" she demanded.

It wasn't the greeting Vicky had hoped for. Instead it was the type that she had feared.

"Could we sit down, Cassie, and talk for a bit?" Vicky asked in a softer voice, hoping to calm Cassie down.

"No, actually we can't. I have a great deal of work to do. To tell you the truth, I'm glad you're alive and that you're obviously okay. Really, I am. But I cannot believe that you would let your family and me think that you had died a long time ago. Surely you must have known that's what we would all think, even if we clung to hope. How many nights did I agonize, did I cry myself to sleep, wondering what had happened to you. Were you hurt? Did you need help? So many questions that I would never be able to find the answers to them all. And yet, apparently I could have, if I'd only known where you were."

"If you'll let me explain…" Vicky began. "I didn't have a choice."

"No, Bobbie, or Vicky or whatever you call yourself. Every single thing we do is a choice. You made a choice to let us all go crazy with fear for you. Then unendurable grief when we finally had to stop denying that you probably had been killed.

You – I guess I never really knew you. The Bobbie that I knew would never have the heart to be that cruel to the people she loved. Sorry. I have work to do." With that, Cassie turned quickly and left the room.

Gram had stood a little bit behind Cassie and she knew better than to try and intervene. The girls would have to work this out for themselves. If they ever could, that is. Gram wondered too, what had happened to Bobbie all those years ago, but she didn't think she should be the first to hear it. "So, have you contacted your mother yet?"

"I still haven't been able to find her. Three months ago when Matt and I came up from Florida, we went first to see his mother. She welcomed us with open arms. Then we went to my old neighborhood and I was surprised to find that my parents had sold the house. A neighbor told me that Mom and Dad had divorced and he had re-married some young chick, as the woman called her, and that she thought Mom eventually had married, too, and moved to the Cape. I told Matt that my number one priority was to find her and after that to find my best friend, Cassie. But no one anywhere seemed to know my mother's new, married name. So we moved down here and I've tried to find it out. So far, unsuccessfully."

Gram started to steer Vicky toward the door. "I will you tell you about your mother. I would expect she'd be overjoyed to see you. Her new name is Bea Willows and her husband is Brian. She seems extremely happy. They live over on Sesuit Harbor in East Dennis." They'd reached Gram's front door, which was on the side of the house. "Vicky, dear, I am happy to see you again. And I hope, in time, Cassie will be, too. Right now she's in shock and she hurts deeply, excruciatingly."

"I know that, Mrs. Barton, and I just hope someday she'll allow me to tell her everything that happened and why we did what we did. Then, if she doesn't want to see me, that's okay. But at least I will have had the opportunity to explain. Perhaps you can tell her that for me." Vicki started down the stairs but stopped at the bottom and looked up. "Mrs. Barton, does this mean you won't be wanting me to coach the girls' softball team at your camp?"

"Nonsense. You're a good coach, I'm sure, and we're lucky to have you. See you at the first practice Thursday afternoon. Will you be ready?"

"Absolutely."

After Vicky left, Gram headed to Cassie's kitchen.

"Janie, dear, have you seen Cassie?"

"Wow, what on earth happened, Gram? She came back in here stomped around, slammed some cabinet doors, she even threw a peach at the wall! Look at that mess she made. I was just about to clean it up. After she did all this, she ran into the office, picked up her purse and shot out of here like a bullet. Never even answered one thing I asked her. Phew – can you tell me what the heck is going on?"

"Oh, dear. She truly is upset. I wish she hadn't gotten behind the wheel of the car like that." Gram heaved a sigh and wondered if she should be telling Janie. The girls not only were partners, but they were best friends and very close. "I'm going to tell you something, but I'd appreciate it if you wouldn't tell anyone else yet. Please let Cassie do it in her own time, all right?"

Janie nodded. "You know her friend, Bobbie, that she's told you about?"

"Of course. That was a terrible story. It was awful what happened to Bobbie. Why do you ask?"

"Because Bobbie Avery is alive. Not only that, she was just here."

Janie's mouth dropped open. "Say that again?" She slid down onto the kitchen stool.

"I had asked around for a softball coach for my girls camp. And one day I was told about a new girl in town that had coached down in Florida. Her name is Vicky Doyle. So I interviewed her. And nearly croaked when she showed up and turned out to be our own Bobbie Avery. Apparently she changed her name a long time ago."

Janie still couldn't quite grasp that this person was really alive – and here! "How did Cassie take

IF YOU FIND ME...

it? Actually I guess not well, considering she came back here and almost tried to demolish the place."

"I'm not sure if she's still in shock. I know right now she's filled with anger and hurt. But I really don't know what will come next. Do you think she'll turn to Ben?"

"Probably," Janie replied. "I hope so."

~~~~~~~~~~~~~~~~~

Cassie drove around and around, not having any clue where she was headed.

Maybe I should go to the beach. No, that's no good. Every tourist on the Cape is at the beach. Then over to the conservation land for a walk. No, I don't feel like walking.

She pulled the car over. Cassie rubbed her forehead. *I don't even know what I'm feeling.* Her mind kept going blank. It truly couldn't process the news.

In the end Cassie decided she needed to see Ben. Carefully, she pulled back out into the traffic. There were cars everywhere. So many people had come down to the Cape for the long holiday over the 4th. She inched along bumper to bumper in the traffic. Across the street, you could see little wavy lines of steam rising from the black pavement. The clouds had gone and the sun reigned in the sky. People were heading to the beach with umbrellas,

141

beach chairs, and inner tubes tied to the tops of their cars.

Cassie pulled up in front of The Pastry Shop. Ben's little bakery was a welcoming beacon on an otherwise busy, touristy road. From first glance, the white, clapboard shop seemed very small but the building went deep into the back of the lot. Two carriage lights adorned the sides of the front door, and little window boxes filled with purple pansies and blue phlox brightened the windows. Wooden cutouts in the shape of muffins decorated the boxes. The minute a customer gets out of the car, the aroma of muffins, bread and more exotic delicacies beckons them in. Cassie felt her shoulders begin to loosen. She got out and went inside.

Ben was so excited at first to see her. But he soon noticed things definitely weren't all right – a tiny tilt of her head to the right, one eyebrow slightly peaked upwards, her pixie hair running askew. Things definitely weren't all right.

"Let's go out back, hon, where we can talk." He motioned to his assistant to take over the counter.

One of the rooms in the back was his den/office and he led Cassie there. Immediately he threw his arms around her.

"You're shaking, Cass. What is it?" He wrapped her tighter in his arms.

She kept repeating the phrase, 'I don't understand,' over and over.

"Sweetheart, take a slow breath. Try and tell me what's happened. Just start out slow. It's okay." He kissed her forehead.

"It's my friend, Bobbie. She's back. She's alive."

Astonished, he asked, "What? Are you certain?"

"She says she changed her name." That was all Cassie could think of to say. She felt numb all over, like someone had pumped her body full of novocaine.

"You're in shock," Ben said, recognizing her glazed look and frozen stance. Any minute he was afraid she would collapse.

"Please, sit here on the couch for one second. I have to get us some cups of coffee."

While he was gone Cassie closed her eyes and replayed the scene in her mind. It didn't change. Bobbie stood there telling her, "My name is Vicky." Why? What possibly could have happened to her that would keep her away all that time? Why would Bobbie have let us all believe she was dead? It just didn't sound like the Bobbie she grew up with. Cassie tried hard to think of something, anything that could have kept her away for ten years. But it was impossible.

When Ben came back she asked him those same questions.

"I can't imagine. Whatever it was, had to be something really huge. From what you've told me of your friend, I would think it would have been extremely painful for her to be away from her family and you for so long a time without being able to get in touch with you."

"What do you mean, 'able?' The girl lived in Florida, Gram said. Believe it or not they do have mail service and even telephones down there," Cassie sarcastically replied.

"How about we take a few sips of this delicious coffee and just sit quiet, holding hands – just for a minute."

Cassie looked at him like he was a lunatic, but decided, why not.

The coffee was good and hot and Ben had made sure there was plenty of sugar in it to help deal with the shock. At least, he thought that's what you did. He also wanted to see if her body could calm down. Oh brother, he thought to himself. Give someone high-test coffee and expect them to calm down. Dope! Oh, well, the funny thing was, it seemed to be working. Soon, Cassie took a very deep breath and let it all out. A little pink hue began to appear on her face.

"Cass, honey. There are a few things I'd like to share with you that I haven't probably said before." Ben picked up her hand in both of his. "You are a woman of great strength. Amazing, really. And it's something that you have that comes from deep inside you. It's like a pool of inner strength that you dip into now and then and you share it with others to help them get through any crisis they face. I've watched you over the years. Rarely have I ever seen you angry. And if you do get upset, it's soon gone, because you stop and think about things. 'Why has something happened, you ask.' And more often than not, you'll want to find out what you can do to help make it better instead of hanging on to your anger." Ben pulled her hand to his lips and kissed it.

Cassie wanted to put her head onto his shoulder and melt into his arms.

"Recently is a good example with Dorrie. Everyone got upset at her, mad, probably some wanted to get even. I know I didn't take her shenanigans too well."

"I was upset, too, you know," Cassie reminded him.

"True. But you didn't leave it there. Even if some of us might have wondered why our friend had changed, only you cared enough to find out why and see what to do to help. That's who you are. And I love you deeply for it. You're a great teacher, Cassie. I'm learning how to handle things in a better way, thanks to you." After a few seconds of silence, Ben continued. "So along comes you're childhood friend who's been lost to you for ten years. This is a miracle, Hon. An honest to goodness miracle. A person you cared for with your heart and soul, and who you thought was surely dead, has come back, alive. This calls for a celebration of life. Do you really care about anything else but the fact that this person so dear to you has come back into your life? Maybe she made a really, really huge mistake in being quiet all these years. And then again, maybe she has an astounding reason why she hasn't even called her mother. But I know this. You were able to forgive Dorrie for everything she's done. Even if it turns out whether she is sick or isn't, you've forgiven her, have you not?"

Cassie nodded her head yes. Soaking up Ben's words, Cassie knew they felt right. Her heart wanted to open to Bobbie.

"This isn't going to happen, okay – but what IF Bobbie vanished again tomorrow. What then?"

Cassie jumped up out of the couch. "OH my goodness! No!"

"Honey, easy. I said it wasn't going to happen. I just wanted you to hear what your heart has been trying to tell you all along. That you love that gal. You always said you were like sisters."

"Ben, you're right. I have to see Bobbie. I mean Vicky. She really is back? I mean, she isn't going to disappear again, is she Ben?"

Ben wondered what trouble he'd conjured up now by even suggesting it. Maybe it hadn't been the right thing to say, but he was getting desperate for Cassie to see where her own heart was already leading her. It had just been her shock that had caused her to react in the way she did.

"Ben, I'm not sure I'm as good as you seem to think I am. That's more than I can live up to. I don't want you to be disappointed in me, but I still think there's some anger, or maybe, I don't know, maybe it's just that I feel hurt."

Ben stood up beside her. "You could never, ever disappoint me. Don't think for a second you could. Doesn't matter to me. Feel angry, upset, whatever you need to feel. But then, like you always do, find out what's behind her actions. Why did she do it. Then see how you feel. You know you still love your friend. You just proved it."

"You're right. I really do want to talk to her."

Ben and Cassie moved outside under the maple tree out back. He had some picnic tables there and they ate tuna sandwiches and drank iced tea and planned the errands that Cassie was supposed to be getting done.

While they were talking, Jill, his assistant came outside.

"Ben, Cassie, I don't know how to tell you guys this. But you know that young college gal that was missing?"

"I don't like the sound of this, Jill," Cassie said.

"I know. It's heartbreaking. They just found her body."

Cassie had her elbows on the picnic table and her hands flew up to cover her face.

"Did they mention Gigi?" she asked quietly.

"Not yet. The police are still talking – it's a bulletin on the tv."

Ben and Cassie packed up and went inside.

"For those of you just joining us, the police chief has just revealed that the body of young Mary Chen was found by campers in the woods near Nickerson State Park. The body was partially buried in a shallow grave. They are calling it murder and asking the public to be vigilant. They said there is no sign of the other missing girl, Georgina Shepherd."

The anchor turned to her co-host. "It certainly sounds similar to the murders of those girls several years ago. They were buried in shallow graves."

"Yes, but they were up in Truro -- their remains were found in partially dug graves in a garden of marijuana plants. Hopefully the police have evidence they are checking through. But one does wonder about the whereabouts of that other man, Carl."

"Let's remind our viewers who he is."

"Yes. Six years ago, in 1970, Tony Costa was convicted of murdering three of the four girls who were found dead. Later, Tony wrote in his unpublished book that he had an accomplice named Carl. As far as we know, this man Carl has never been found or brought to justice. So now, we have to ask, where is Carl? Stay tuned for updates."

The phone rang. A second later Jill yelled over to Ben, "It's your Dad."

"Hi Dad. We just heard. It's awful. I sure hope they have good people investigating this now. Oh, he is? That's great news. Uh huh. Good. Listen, I'm going out with Cassie now to help pick up the rest of the stuff they need for the Cook-Off tomorrow. I'll tell her. All right, talk to you later."

Cassie and Jill both looked at him expectantly.

"Dad says that Sean, his F.B.I. agent buddy has arrived and is now taking over the case."

"Oh dear. How does that sit with the local gendarmes?" Cassie asked.

"Dad said they all seemed relieved. It was becoming a jurisdictional nightmare. Mary Chen went missing at the college in Barnstable. Her body was found in Brewster. Gigi Shepherd went missing from the mall, Hyannis. And Christine White, the doc's assistant went missing, possibly from Brewster but they don't know where she was abducted from yet. So they are all delighted to hand it over to the Feds to sort out. Each of the heads of the local police are happy to help as long as someone else is in the driver's seat."

Jill smiled. "Yeah, now all those guys can blame your Dad's friend if something goes wrong. Just what they needed was a fall guy and along he comes!"

"So cynical, so young," Cassie commented to

Jill. "Tsk, tsk. Have you no faith, little one?"

"Oh go ahead, mock me. But you'll see if anything goes wrong. Our local guys will come out on top."

"That may be true, Jill," Ben replied, "but with Sean O'Hara conducting this investigation, ain't nothing going to go wrong."

"We hope!" Cassie and Jill shouted in unison.

After Cassie and Ben left the bakery she told him that they needed to get a supply of paper plates, napkins, plastic forks, and insulated cups for the hot coffee. "Oh, and celery."

"That sounds like a trip to the grocery store," Ben said.

"Say Cassie, do you want to stop in and see Dorrie at her shop?"

Just another tiny reminder of why Cassie loved Ben. She told him it was a wonderful idea and they headed to her place. Dorrie's Delectable Delights was in West Yarmouth, just down the road a piece. When they drove up, Cassie was struck by the fact that there were only two cars present. She expected a madhouse of people and activity, scurrying to get ready for tomorrow just like they were trying to do.

"Dorrie?" she called inside the door.

"Cassie, is that you?" came the reply from the next room. Dorrie peeked her head around a doorway. "Come on back here. I want you to meet my folks."

Dorrie's parents were both older, perhaps even near seventy, Cassie thought. And just so warm and friendly.

Dorrie told her Mom that it was Cassie who helped her decide to make major changes in her life.

"I did?" Cassie asked, surprised.

They talked awhile and Dorrie told them that she had let everybody go yesterday after she'd had a professional auditor come in and exam the books and the business. "Those kids were stealing money from the business, cheating customers, and using my name to pilfer clients out from under every one of my catering friends. And please, Cassie, I hope you'll accept my apology. I was mortified to learn that this had been going on while I've been tuning out for the past month."

Ben asked, "If you don't mind my asking, what happened at the dinner for Richard Price? I still can't believe it went down like it did."

"That one I REALLY regret," Dorrie replied. "My assistant had set that up with Mr. Price. Decided on her own that the big shot could have a chicken dinner instead of lobsters and pocketed the difference in price herself. My lawyer thinks I should press charges against her, but it depends on what Richard Price wants to do. I'm scheduled to talk with him tomorrow." Dorrie shook her head. "But it comes down to being my fault. I wasn't paying any attention to the business. There's no way anyone could have gotten away with that last year. Or even six months ago. I've just been feeling so awful. And so afraid to find out what's wrong. But you helped me change that, Cassie. Thanks."

"Does that mean you're going to see the doctor again?"

"Already did. Yesterday afternoon and he sent me right over to the hospital for a cat scan."

Dorrie's Mom stood up and went over to her daughter, putting her hand on Dorrie's shoulder. Dorrie was sitting in a wing back chair. Standing above her daughter where she couldn't see her Mom, Mrs. St. John quietly shed a few tears.

Oh no, Cassie thought to herself. Please not bad news.

"It's a tumor, guys. I guess I should've had the cat scan last year when I first started getting these headaches, but the doctor said it might not have shown up enough at that time for them to see."

"Are they going to remove it soon?" Ben asked.

"Well, on Thursday I go up to Boston to Mass General for a complete work-up. If all the signs are good, they'll schedule it for Friday."

"Oh my goodness, that's so soon." Cassie was totally surprised at how quickly this all happened. She couldn't imagine what Dorrie must be feeling. "What about tomorrow, Dor?"

Mrs. St. John spoke up. "Her father and I are trying to talk her into at least doing a small booth at the Cook-Off. We're going to stay and help."

"Anything we can do to help, we will," Ben offered.

"You know what, Dorrie, let's set our booths up next to each other and then we can help each other out. What did you have in mind for serving?"

Dorrie laughed. "You'll think I'm nuts but I want to cater to the kids. I want to have a peanut butter, marshmallow, jelly bonanza. Offer all sorts and kinds – almond butter, cashew butter, as well as homemade peanut butter, marshmallow, apple butter, all kinds of jellies and jams. A couple different kinds of breads or rolls. And something that kids would love to drink but I don't want to serve tonic. The association is going to have coke machines everywhere."

Cassie thought a minute. "You know that kids' punch you make when you do birthday parties? The one with the fruit punch, gingerale, orange juice and whatever else you throw in it?"

"Yeah?"

"You can use our champagne fountain and instead of champagne, fill it with the punch. The kids might get a kick out of filling their cups from the fountain as it sprays punch everywhere. You use it and just return it clean and that's it."

"Oh, honey," Mrs. St. John said, "I can see why you told us that Cassie is a special person. Thank you, my dear. Sounds like fun, doesn't it, Dorrie?"

Dorrie nodded her head yes. Her emotions were running toward full to overflowing and didn't think she could speak yet.

It was decided that they'd all meet up at the field tonight at five o'clock. The two groups had decided to merge and set up their booths together so they could all help each other. Dorrie had told them that she wasn't interested in competing for the prize. In fact, when she recuperated from the surgery, she wanted to scale down her business immensely and just handle children's parties.

Cassie was so happy to hear that she had a goal to work toward after her surgery.

From there Ben and Cassie finally did their assigned shopping errands and eventually ended up back at Cassie's place.

"Hey you guys," Janie called. "You missed Sean's first press conference. It was awfully short but he said that Mary Chen had been strangled. She wasn't killed in the woods and they don't know yet where it did happen or who took her. He said they are investigating many leads and that anyone with information about Mary's activities the last two weeks of her life, to come forward."

"Let's hope someone comes up with a name of someone who had been interested in her or mad at her or something," Cassie commented.

"Or stalking her?" Jane asked, looking at Cass.

"If my stalker is Lenny Marek, I'm telling you

he's harmless. Okay? Besides, I haven't seen him in days."

Ben left to go back to work and the girls began to prepare what they could for the next day. The plan was for everyone to meet at the field at five o'clock – Cassie had filled Jane and the girls in on Dorrie. Janie and Sam were excited about helping Dorrie. Another two converts to the, "help instead of yell" group. Bonnie said she'd reserve judgment until tonight. She wanted to make sure this new Dorrie was really genuine. Cassie thought of the story of doubting Thomas in the Bible, but refrained from pointing it out. Bonnie was young and she was doubly hurt thanks to Jessica.

Ben and his Dad, Kevin and Tim, and a whole lot of other people were going to be on hand to help set up the booth and get everything ready for tomorrow. Then the plan was to gather back at Cassie's. While they were all gone, Gram and Cassie's Mom, Shirley, were going to get a big dinner ready for everyone. Gram said they would need lots of good carbohydrates and protein for the big day tomorrow.

~~~~~~~~~~~~~

"There's a call for you on line one."

He groaned. It's too early, though. It's probably not him. Crossing his fingers he picked up the phone.

"You get the package yet?"

"No. You gave me until Friday, remember?"

"Don't get excited. I'm offering you another way out. You can do this new job instead of the other one. Your choice."

He thought a minute.

"What is it?" he asked warily.

After Louis Balboni told him the job he had for him to do, he started sputtering and choking.

"NO – uh -uh- no -no -NO WAY. You said I had a choice. I want the other job back – finding that package you want."

"Too late. This is your job now."

"You said I had a choice!"

"Listen, moron – you play with the big guys – the stakes are high. This ain't kids cops and robbers. You're my stooge now and you do what I say. Remember – it really comes down to this – you complete this job or you might as well say good-bye folks. Oh, and by the way, the client hiring us for this job – he wants it done tomorrow at that big event on the Cape in Yarmouth. There will be a lot of people around. Should make it easier. Here's the details."

After he hung up, he ran into the bathroom and threw up all over the place. Now what do I do?

~~~~~~~~~~~~~~~~~

Everyone piled into the Conservatory and took seats at the big table that had been set up.

Bonnie and Sam helped Gram and Shirley bring in the dinner -- lasagna, salad, and fresh zucchini from the garden. Along with warm Italian bread that Ben had baked earlier. Cassie's Dad opened a bottle of Rosé.

And when all fifteen of them were seated, Cassie asked if it was all right with everyone if they could say grace. She made it short but heartfelt.

Afterwards, she said, "I want to thank each one of you for all your help. It certainly made it easier this afternoon to get all set up for tomorrow."

Janie hit the wine glass with her knife, yelling, "Here, here! Thanks everyone – we sure make a great team!"

"I guess that sums it up then. Let's eat!"

The quiet hum of friends eating together filled the room. The crystal chandelier shed a delicate light over the dinner. Outside the tiny white lights flickered around like fireflies as the breeze tossed the branches up and down.

"I asked Sean to join us when he gets free. He's formed a task force to investigate Mary Chen's murder and the disappearance of Gigi Shepherd and Christine White."

"That's great, Tom, thanks," Cassie said.

Shortly after that Sean arrived.

"Wow, does that smell incredible!" he said the

minute he came into the room.

Cassie introduced everyone while he took the empty seat left for him. She let him eat for awhile before starting her interrogation.

"Is there anything you're allowed to tell us, Sean?" she finally asked, unable to wait longer.

"As a matter of fact, there is one important clue that we're hoping will lead us to the suspect. At the scene, there was a boot print found near the body." Sean stopped and looked around. "You know maybe I better wait til dinner is finished. I promise to tell you more then, okay?"

"Thank you, Agent O'Hara," Gram said. "I know we are all anxious to hear of your progress but not at the expense of our appetite."

"Of course, Mrs. Barton. I totally agree."

Dessert was a heavenly fresh baked blueberry pie with ice cream, that Gram had made, or lemon meringue pie that Ben had made and brought with him.

Actually, they both had made two of each and by the time everyone was done there wasn't a slice of anything left.

"Um, excuse me?" This small voice said.

Cassie barely recognized the voice as Dorrie's.

She nodded encouragement to her friend.

"I just want to thank each of you for everything you are doing to help me. From this glorious dinner – thank you so much Mrs. Barton and Mrs. Wood –

to the help at the field. I feel incredibly blessed to have such generous friends and I'm very excited about tomorrow thanks to all of you."

Janie started clapping and the rest joined in.

"Our prayers will be with you Friday, Dorrie. And when you get back on the Cape after your surgery, we're going to throw you a big party. Is that okay?"

"Sounds fantastic!"

Everyone pitched in clearing the table and helping out in the kitchen. Cassie suggested that Dorrie and her parents call it a night. She could tell Dorrie felt tired. "Thanks, Cassie. I really do want to rest up for the big day tomorrow. You're the best," she said, hugging her friend.

Several of the others left, too. Cassie sent Bonnie, Sam, and Tim along home with instructions to be back bright and early. Kevin wanted to stay with Janie and listen to what Sean had to say. But Cassie's parents bid everyone good night, as did Gram.

The rest were getting a hot drink to bring into the Conservatory so they could sit down and chat.

"Janie, you've probably had about eight cups of coffee today. You want to drink some of this orange and rose hip tea so you can slow your body down a little?" Cassie asked.

"I'll drink orange, green, white, even purple tea if you want, but not until this summer is over!"

Janie replied. "There's an equation that goes, one must have coffee of equal strength to the amount of stress one is enduring. Coffee, folks. Not herbal tea." With that, she loaded cream and sugar into her coffee mug and marched back to the Conservatory.

"She made that up, right?" Cassie asked Ben.

"Beats me, but that gal is flying. I don't know how she's going to quiet down to sleep later."

Eventually they were all set and gave Sean the floor.

"Okay, so I mentioned the boot print. It's from a military issue boot. The boot print is nice and clear and had to have been put there after the rain stopped or it would've been washed away. So that gives us a general time. Of course the young woman was killed elsewhere and then transported to the place where she was found. We're not sure the significance of that yet."

"If it's military, there isn't really a way to track who it belonged to, is there. And think of all the vets now back from the Vietnam War. There's no way. How is it helpful?" Ben asked.

"Well, for one. Boot size gives us foot size and the depth of the impression gives us a possible weight of the suspect. We figure we're looking for someone who weighs approximately one hundred-seventy pounds and has a size twelve foot. That's more than we had before."

Cassie piped up, "What type of ligature was

used to strangle her? Does that give us a clue?"

"Who said anything about a ligature."

"Don't tell me Mary Chen was strangled with someone's bare hands? Is that even possible?"

"Only someone of great strength. Someone particularly aggressive and full of anger. She wasn't a tiny girl and there were signs she fought her attacker. But so far we're not finding anyone in her life with that type of rage."

Janie sipped her coffee and jumped out of her seat and started pacing the floor.

Cassie remembered when she first met Janie. She'd been working at the Boston caterer for two years when Janie got a job with them. She was fresh out of high school and three years younger than Cassie. The young Janie hadn't outgrown that tomboy phase that many young girls go through. Plus the youngster had grown up in Dorchester in one of the rougher, poorer sections. There had never been any talk of college in her household. She told Cassie her parents would have laughed at her or more likely screamed at her, she'd said, when she thought about going to college. So Janie never brought it up. Her grades were slightly above average, not good enough for a scholarship. But her grandmother had been a great cook and Janie loved helping her. It had been a huge blow when her grandmother passed away. Janie was only fourteen then.

The minute Jane graduated from high school her parents told her she had to get a job and start paying room and board or move out. After a month when Cassie and Janie had become close friends, Cassie had asked her if she wanted to move into her apartment with her. Janie wasn't sure she could swing it, but Cassie made sure to make it affordable for the young girl. Their apartment was in the Back Bay in an old building with a creaking elevator. The girls kept their figures thin in those couple years, from walking up the four flights of stairs. They just didn't trust that rattle-trap cage of an elevator. Cassie thought of all the fun they'd had when Cass would take Jane to places she'd never been – the Museum of Fine Arts, the Museum of Science, a play at the Wilbur theater. None of the things had Janie ever seen and she was like a little bird first learning to fly.

Unfortunately Janie didn't grow up with a warm and loving family like Cassie did, so Jane wasn't real surprised when her parents told her she needed to start sending them part of her pay check. They had supported her all those years, now it was her turn to support them. Janie could barely make ends meet. It was Cassie who paid for all their outings and for most of the food. She didn't care, she loved seeing the joy that Janie got from everything.

After Cassie had been there four years, and Janie for two, that was when Cassie had gotten the idea to start the business on Cape Cod. Gram and her parents had already retired to the Cape and Cassie thought it a great idea to join them. And there was never a question – Cassie wanted to take Janie with her. But she wondered if Janie wanted to go.

Cassie needn't have worried. Janie said she could pack and be ready in fifteen minutes. Just let her know which day they were moving. When Janie turned twenty-one she discovered that her grandmother had left a trust for her to start paying out to Jane when she turned twenty-one. So Janie took enough to buy into the business as a junior partner and here they were today. Over the years Cassie watched Janie gain a little more confidence with time and experience. But when she asked Cassie the other night about dating Kevin, Cassie was surprised at how scared Janie was. She didn't know what to do. She really liked him a lot. He was the first boy she ever cared for. Considering that Jane was now twenty-four it was kind of surprising. Cassie had answered any of the questions she could and then told Jane to relax and just have fun. Then Cassie turned around and had a talk with her cousin, Kevin. If he ever hurt Janie, she'd told him, Cassie would hunt him down and it wouldn't be pretty. Kev promised to take fantastic care of Janie. "You know something, Cassie, I honestly think I'm in love with Jane. I don't know if she's ready to hear that yet, but I'm positively crazy about her.

Isn't she the best?" Then Cassie knew her dear friend was in good hands.

So tonight when Janie had jumped up and started pacing, Cassie wondered if it was from the coffee or something more.

"Janie, hon, what's up?" she asked.

"I wish there was something we could do! It's frustrating, knowing Gigi is out there somewhere and Christine, and we can't seem to do anything to help. Like this boot print thing, should someone be going to the army/navy store in Hyannis and ask if any guys bought boots like that recently? I mean, could you even tell from the tread if the boot is old or not?" she asked Sean.

"That's an excellent question, Jane. As a matter of fact, the boot tread was very worn. After we did plaster casts, I inspected the print itself for foreign matter and actually found granules of sand."

Cassie and Ben laughed. "That's not so odd considering that Cape Cod is basically one big sand dune," Cassie commented.

"That's true but this sand had gravel mixed with it."

"And what does that tell you?" Ben asked.

Sean shook his head. "Maybe not a heck of a lot. But when we have a suspect, then we have something to match up with. Also it tells us this person's location previous to those woods, was a sandy, gravelly place. Oh, and Janie, that comment about the army/navy store? We did go there and talk to the manager. He gave us a list of regulars that come in and either sell him some of their army equipment or buy other stuff from him. The man said that some of these vets were homeless."

Heads nodded, but several loud yawns were heard as well. Cassie looked at her watch.

"Oh my goodness. Look at the time. It's already after eleven p.m. Perhaps we should call it a night. Most of us have a very early start tomorrow. But I want to thank you gentlemen for helping out so much."

They all said their goodnight, even Ben. Cassie was just too tired to stay up any longer. After they all left, she suggested to Janie a little warm milk before bed, something to calm Janie's coffee jitters.

After finishing her milk, Janie asked, "Cassie, what do you think is going to happen tomorrow?" A few yawns followed her question.

"I think we're going to work our little tails off and have a whole bunch of fun doing it, don't you?"

Janie nodded, yawned, and started trudging toward the stairs. By the time they reached the top, she was practically sleepwalking to her room.

Cassie hugged her, watched her get safely to her room then joined Middy and ended up having a dreamless, beautiful night's sleep.

And then the fourth of July dawned, and life was about to be turned upside down.

Wednesday, July 4, 1976

CHAPTER JEVEN

A sign hung over the entrance to the recreational field at the Yarmouth elementary school that read:

HAPPY FOURTH OF JULY!
WELCOME TO THE CAPE COD CATERER'S
COOK-OFF
sponsored by the
CAPE COD VOLUNTEERS' ASSOCIATION

The perfect weather held on for the fourth of July celebrations. Puffy white clouds dotted the marine blue sky, the sun was shining and a breeze sailed in off the ocean. At noontime the fair came to life with activity -- there were youngsters having their faces painted by clowns, carnival booths where throwing rubber rings or bean bags meant winning prizes, a big white tent held tables of crafts for sale, items made by volunteers and members of the Yarmouth and Dennis women's clubs. The garden club had plants, seeds and flower arrangements for sale. In another part of the field children's games were underway — three-legged races and tug of war. And of course, the all important caterers' booths with yummy items to eat.

Cassie's Cuisine and Dorrie's Party Time were nestled together in the shade of a big evergreen tree, the best spot on the field. Unless you wanted to bake in the heat, which none of them did. Dorrie had changed the name of her business to reflect the new direction, parties for kids. Cassie's seafood rolls were a huge hit. Ben had convinced her to use finger rolls instead of roll-ups. Even though they didn't hold as much seafood filling, they didn't cost as much which turned out to be a great idea. Folks loved them.

Every where you turned people were laughing and having a great time. At one point Cassie thought she saw Joe Picoli, but she didn't look too closely. If he was here, she definitely wanted to keep her distance.

Just after the lunchtime rush of madness, Cassie was staring out into the crowd when she saw Bobbie, or rather Vicky, standing beside a young girl and a handsome man. Cassie pointed them out to Ben. He was glad to see how excited she was. Reassuring her that they had everything under control at the booth, Ben urged her to go see them.

Vicky had seen Cassie looking their way. She wasn't sure what she should do. With all her heart, Vicky wanted a chance to tell Cassie the whole story of what happened back then. But Cassie had made it pretty clear last time that she didn't care about the reasons. Vicky knew that Cassie had been deeply hurt and it pained Vicky to think about how horrible it must have been for those she left behind. So Vicky waited and pondered. To her surprise, she saw Cassie leave the booth and head her way. Oh boy, Vicky thought, is she coming over here to scream at me? She didn't want her little girl to hear someone yelling at her Mommy, but a little corner of her heart held out hope that Cassie might feel differently today.

"Hi Vicky," Cassie said warmly.

"Hi."

"If I'm real nice do I get to meet your lovely family?" Cassie asked timidly.

Vicky's face broke out in a huge smile.

"You bet. This little gal is my daughter Sandy and she's seven years old."

"Hi!" Sandy said, putting her hand out.

Cassie shook it. "I like your name. It's similar to mine. I'm Cassandra."

"Oh Mommy! She's the one, isn't she." Sandy looked at Cassie and said, "I'm named for you!"

Cassie's mouth fell open. She looked at Vicky.

"It's true, Cass. Sandy's real name is Cassandra but we couldn't call her Cassie. We were told it would be too dangerous, that certain people might recognize the name and put two and two together."

"What?" Cassie asked.

"Oh man. It's a long story. I don't suppose you have time right now."

"Actually I do," Cassie responded because this was more important at the moment than anything else she should be doing.

"Oh, forgive me, dear," Vicky said to her husband. "This is my husband, Matthew Doyle. You may have seen his byline in the Cape Cod Times."

"Yes, of course. You do features. Your style is very lyrical. I enjoy reading your columns."

"You're very kind, Cassie, thank you. Vicky, why don't I take Sandy and go see which one of the carnival games we can win next."

"Ooh, I want to win the pony, Dad," Sandy replied with a huge, missing-teeth grin.

By way of explanation, Matt said, "There's a rather large stuffed pony as one of the prizes at the bean bag game. You have to knock down seven bottles to win it."

"You can do it, Daddy, I know you can."

Vicky turned to him. "Go be a hero. Cassie and I are going to get caught up."

After they'd left, Cassie suggested they move over to the picnic tables in the shade and they picked up some lemonade on the way.

"I have so many questions, I don't even know where to start," Cassie began.

"Then is it okay if I just tell it like a story, starting at the beginning? And you can stop and ask questions as we go?"

Cassie nodded her head, anxious to hear what happened in Bobbie's life to change the universe upside down for them both.

"Do you remember back in the fall of our senior year that I used to go into Boston with my brother Jack on Saturdays fairly often?"

Cassie thought back and remembered. "They used to have parties on Saturdays, right? I kept wishing my folks would let me go with you to one of them."

"I know. I was surprised they didn't with Jack there. But I guess, to be fair, he looked like quite the dope smoking hippie that he was. Not much to inspire parental confidence. Now that I'm a mother, believe me, I understand a whole lot better."

Cassie chuckled.

"So these parties were at the apartment where Jack and three of his buddies lived. One of those guys was a handsome college senior – he was in some of the same classes at Emerson with Jack. Anyway, his name, at that time was Tony, and his uncle was Nicky Balboni, head of the crime syndicate in Atlantic City, New Jersey. Uncle Nicky wanted Tony to go into the family business and start preparing to take over. Tony's own father, Anthony Balboni, had been the head of their operations first, but he'd been killed by a local gang member trying to make a name for himself. So Uncle decided that Tony was the next heir to the business. Tony didn't want anything to do with it. He refused. At first Uncle Nicky sent him gifts and money, too, but Tony didn't want any part of it and sent everything back.

"Apparently this made Uncle very mad. All through that last year at college Tony kept looking over his shoulder. The other thing Uncle didn't like – was me. He told Tony to dump me, that I wasn't "family" material.

"Right before I ran away, I had visited Tony the week-end before. We had just come out of the apartment building and were almost at his car, when it exploded."

Cassie gasped.

"The wave knocked us both back onto the pavement. Other than scrapes and bruises we were okay, just thoroughly shaken. While trying to pick each other up, a thug in a fedora walked over to us. He said, 'Hey kids, that was close, huh?' Then he took out a gun and started waving it at us. The thing was so big it looked like a bazooka!"

"I can't believe you're smiling while you're telling me this," Cassie remarked. "The terror you must have felt! It takes my breath away just thinking about it."

"Crazy, huh? Ten years is a long time to think

about things that happened and try to put our lives in perspective. I think we've done pretty good until this year. But that comes later." Vicky sighed. She was surprised to feel the darkness come crawling back as she thought about the next part. Trying not to let it get to her, Vicky continued. "The Thug is still standing there, waving the gun, and he says, 'So, Tony, just so we're clear. That little demonstration was a message from Uncle Nicky. Either you toe the line and report for work, or get ready to swim with the fishes. You too, dearie,' he'd said, patting my cheek and walking away."

Now Vicky shivered. That part of the story still had the power to frighten her. Especially now that they had their daughter to protect as well. Unexpectedly, her body started rocking. Cassie reached across the picnic table and closed her hands around Vicky's. They were freezing. Cassie couldn't believe it in the middle of a hot summer day, Vicky's hands felt like they'd been soaking in an ice bucket.

"I couldn't breathe," Vicky continued. "Not from the explosion, but from fear. Pure deep, pulsating fear that oozed through every pore in my body. We could have been killed! The coldness of it, like it was just a whim of Uncle Nicky's whether we lived or died. I don't think the guy was right when he said Uncle Nicky wanted Tony to take over the business. Things had gone beyond that.

Obviously, he wanted us dead. Period."

Vicky heaved a deep sigh. "That was it, the turning point. Neither one of us felt safe trying to stay, not even long enough to finish out our senior year – his or mine. Staying meant only one thing – finding out just how Uncle Nicky planned to kill us. I hope you can understand, Cassie, how incredibly scared we were. Uncle Nicky wasn't playing nice anymore. We took off and never looked back. We just kept driving until one day we realized we had made it to Florida. But in order to feel safe, we decided we had to completely change our identities. Who knows just how far Uncle Nick would go to get rid of us."

Vicky stopped and took a swig of the lemonade. It was refreshing and she needed to wet her mouth so she could continue.

"After we'd been there for three years, we had our wonderful daughter, Sandy. Everything seemed to be going well, but we both missed our families and friends more and more. Then, six months ago, Uncle Nicky died and we hoped it finally meant we could come home. We had been living in constant fear that people we knew and loved might be hurt in order to flush us out of hiding, but thank goodness it never happened.

"Uncle Nicky left the family business to the last remaining brother, Louis Balboni. He's also an uncle of Tony's, or Matthew, as we call him now.

We made the name changes legally in court when we first moved to Florida. So three months' ago we made the trip back up north and here we are. We're still afraid that Louie might come after us. Surely he wants to run the business himself. Matt says it's a combination of things – first, Uncle Louie doesn't want Matt changing his mind and trying to take over the family business, and second, it's a matter of honor or some such stupid macho thing. So, here we are, still alive and trying to stay that way. What do you think?"

Vicky kept her fingers crossed under the table, hoping for Cassie's approval or at least her understanding.

"Oh Vicky, you've been through so much. It's unbelievable and now I can completely understand why you did the things that you did. It took courage for you both to uproot your lives and leave everyone and everything behind. And I can't imagine the fear you felt." Cassie reached over and threw her arms around Vicky.

"I really hated what my disappearing must be doing to my family and to you. I'd burst into tears. But Matt had talked with an F.B.I. agent before we ran and one of the things the guy said was, 'If you run, don't ever get in touch with anyone from the past or it could bring harm to them or to you.' He stressed that. Of course he also tried to talk us into staying and testifying against Uncle Nicky but Matt believed that we wouldn't be safe. Oh and I might have left out one kind of big, really big detail."

Cassie's eyes widened. "What could that be?"

"Before we left, Matt said he wanted some insurance. I found out later that he had stolen Nicky Balboni's record book. Names, dates, jobs, money laundering, contract killings – you name it – the idiot had written it all down."

"Holy cow!" Cassie shouted. "Do you guys still have it?"

"We put it in a safe place and when the time comes we'll turn it over to the F.B.I. We're tired of running, Cassie. I hope we'll finally be able to put it all to rest. Your nice agent, Sean, maybe he's the one that Matt will be able to trust. I hope so."

"I hope so, too."

Both girls were quiet a minute, then Vicky spoke again.

"You know, I had this mental game that I played. Remember when we were kids and you were so good at finding lost pets and things?"

"Yup, I remember. I always thought I'd end up some kind of investigator."

"Well, on days when I was feeling down, and missing everyone, I'd play this game. I'd say: 'Cassie, IF YOU FIND ME...' then I'd fill in the blank. Like, If you find me, then I can come home and we can go out dancing. Or another time it would be, If you find me, then I can come home and we can go to the movies. I used to make up all kinds of things we could do together. Things we should have been able to do together but were never able to. You know, I always thought that if anyone could find us, it would be you."

"Believe me, I tried. Really, really tried, Bobbie. Every day I spent some time looking, or calling and asking questions, I must have made thousands of calls especially those first six months. Finally it was Gram that put a stop to it. She said I was losing too much weight and was getting sick. She helped me find that job at the caterer in Boston and that led me to where I am today. And I can tell you, Vicky, that I'm extremely happy. Well, even happier now that I have you back!"

The girls had so much they wanted to hear about each other, but Vicky fretted about being away from Sandy and Matt so long, and Cassie felt she should return to work. They decided on a stop up at the ladies' room in the school, and they'd made a luncheon date for later in the week. All was well, and Cassie felt better than she had in months.

~~~~~~~~~~~~~~~~

Back at the booths, Cassie's Cuisine and Dorrie's Party Time, business was brisk but manageable. Kevin was pouring more fruit punch into the champagne fountain. The kids were loving it. He got a kick out of watching them fill their paper cups with purple punch spurting from the fountain and getting it all over themselves. Janie loved watching Kevin. He had a James Dean look about him. Seeing him interact with the children brought a smile to her face. A few minutes later Ben caught sight of them holding hands. He checked on all of them – Bonnie and Sam were having a great time waiting on folks. Earlier, Dorrie had looked a little pale, but he had given her a couple of the seafood rolls to eat and she seemed to pick up nicely. Ben had walked around a little earlier and enjoyed some of the carnival atmosphere. He had run across Richard Price and they chatted a few minutes. But mostly Ben stayed at the booths watching over things, helping out, waiting until Cassie and he could meander through the crowd together. He had something important on his mind and could barely suppress his excitement, anticipating, hoping what her answer would be.

"Dorrie, dear?" Her Mom called. "We need more of that plum jam. The kids are loving it. Do you feel up to walking to the refrigerated truck and getting some?"

"Absolutely. I don't want to just sit around and watch you guys do all the work. I want to have some of the fun, too!"

"Thanks, honey."

Dorrie had gotten so thin and pale, and she tired

easily. Her Mom worried about her, but Dorrie was a trooper. With her whole heart, Mrs. St. John trusted that God would be with them through this surgery and recovery. She held a unique view of the world. Shelly St. John believed that the surgeon, doctors and nurses, were being guided by God to carry out His healing work, to bring her beloved daughter through this in the most perfect and best way. Dorrie's Mom didn't wear rose-colored, Pollyana-type glasses, she just believed in turning to God and asking to be a channel for His goodness and grace to work through us. Now, in her seventies, looking back over the years, Shelly St. John knew that her faith had helped bring her and her family through so many things, just as it would now.

The communal truck was in the parking lot about fifty feet away. Dorrie thought the exercise would do her some good. She wasn't exactly watching where she was going, part of her brain was busy thinking about the surgery in two days' time. Dorrie wanted very badly to make it through this. It would be her chance to start all over. Plus she had a feeling there were a few fences that she needed to mend after her employees caused so much havoc. She couldn't believe that her assistant, whose voice sounded just like Dorrie's, had pretended to be Dorrie when she was stealing clients our from under Dorrie's friends. Dorrie knew she had to let go of her anger. She wanted only positive thoughts and energy going into her surgery.

When Dorrie stopped to pick up some trash on the ground, Louie Balboni's stooge jumped out from behind a bush wearing a ski mask and brandishing a knife. Dorrie hadn't seen it coming. She screamed.

He truly had agonized over this 'new' job that Mr. Balboni told him he had to do. He just didn't want to do it. He wasn't even sure that he could follow through. Maybe if he made it look good – like he had tried but failed – maybe that would be good enough. Maybe Mr. Balboni would forgive his loan, money he took to get his restaurant started and never paid back, and that led him deeper and deeper in debt to the man. So maybe Louie would tell him he didn't have to pay it back. And maybe, he thought, snowflakes will fall from the sky tonight, right before the fourth of July fireworks. Right.

So here he was trying to make it look good, but not actually hurt Dorrie. After he grabbed her, he tentatively struck her left arm with the knife, then ran. But as he pushed by her, he accidentally knocked her down. Oh no, sorry, he thought. He felt bad about not stopping to help her or make sure that she was all right. His mind was all confused so he just ran. Thirty yards away he threw the ski mask and knife in the wastebasket and kept running at full speed. Eventually he stopped and had no idea what to do next. Without a plan he decided he might as well go back into the crowd at the field. After all, there really was no where for him to run. Where was he going to run to? And when was it going to end? Never.

Shortly after she'd been hit, Dorrie started yelling for help. She hoped she wouldn't pass out from loss of blood before help arrived.

Back at the booths, Dorrie's Mom started to miss her.

"Say Ben, I sent Dorrie to go get some jam off the truck quite awhile ago and she hasn't come back. I'd think if she was going to wander around she would have brought it back first. I hope she's all right."

"Don't you fear, Mrs. St. John, I'll just go and see if I can help her."

"Thank you, dear."

Ben thought Dorrie's parents were incredible. They had pitched right in and were being a really big help.

Picking out a path that led toward the truck, Ben walked along slowly in the heat. He thought probably Dorrie had gone to the ladies' room but where she was so sick, he knew they'd all feel better once she reappeared. Soon he heard a pitiful cry for help. Ben ran up to Dorrie. Seeing all that blood scared him but he yanked his handkerchief out of his pocket and wrapped it tightly around the wound. Then he started screaming at the top of his lungs. His screech brought quite a number of people running, including the paramedics.

Before they whisked her away in the ambulance, the police questioned her thoroughly while the paramedics worked on her arm. They were amazed at the details she remembered. Dorrie described exactly what the man had been wearing – jeans, black sneakers, a black t-shirt, a brown leather belt, and in his right hand he held the knife. On his right wrist she saw a gold watch. And oh yes, she finally remembered to tell them, "I scratched his arm and it drew blood." Patrolmen were ordered to search the crowd and locate her attacker.

The man, the 'stooge,' decided he was tired of having Louis Balboni's threats hanging over him. Dope that he was, it finally sunk in that Louie was never going to let him go. There would always be something he wanted him to do, either that or Louie would have him killed for botching this job. After all, the client paid to have Dorrie St. John killed, not injured. So he did the only smart thing he could think of. He walked up to a guy wearing a white button down shirt and tie. The man was the only one dressed that way. He had to be either a detective or F.B.I. And he turned himself in.

~~~~~~~~~~~~~~~~~~~~

After the ambulance left, with Dorrie's Mom also inside, the police asked Ben some questions, but he happened on the scene after the attacker had left. All this activity took a great deal of time.

At some point, Ben became aware that Cassie had been missing for close to two hours. That didn't sound like Cassie. Even if she and her friend were having a great time catching up with one another, Cassie still would have checked in by now to make sure things were running smoothly. Ben grew uneasy and mentioned it to his Dad.

"I agree, Ben. I think I'll take a look around. Maybe Shirley, Cassie's Mom would like to join me."

"I'm coming, too. Janie and Gram and the girls can work the booths for a bit, it's not too busy right now."

Tom said, "Okay, and Sean is going to try and stop by sometime if he has a free minute from the investigation. Not that we're going to need him," Tom reassured his son.

All of a sudden Ben wasn't so sure. And it scared him to death.

They were just starting off when Ben spied Vicky with her daughter and husband coming out of the crafts' tent. Oh no, oh no, he kept repeating it in his mind as he was running up to them, weaving in and out of the crowd. He hoped he didn't lose sight of them.

Nearly out of breath, he called, "Vicky? My name is Ben."

"Of course. Cassie told me all about you."

"I'm sorry to interrupt, but do you know where Cassie is?"

Vicky looked puzzled. "Didn't she go back to the booth? That's where she was headed. We had gone up into the school to use the ladies' room and when we came back out I saw my husband and daughter from the stairs. Cassie and I said goodbye and I went in their direction while Cassie headed toward your booth."

"Can you show us the route?" Tom asked.

A commotion nearby caught Ben's eye.

"Hey Dad, look! There's Sean. I'll go get him and meet you over near the school."

Ben ran over to where Sean was handing someone over to the local police.

"Sean!"

"Hey Ben. I bet you know this guy."

The 'guy' turned around.

"Joe? Joe Picoli?"

"Hi Ben. I'd shake your hand but as you can see..." He lifted up his arms, showing the handcuffs around his wrists.

"What on earth?" Ben asked.

"Mr. Picoli here is the one who stabbed Dorrie."

Ben looked at Joe in disbelief. For one thing, Ben barely recognized him. The scruffy facial hair showed how unkempt he was, not at all the dapper young restauranteur with the gigantic ego that Ben was used to. That's when he took in the black t-shirt and jeans that Dorrie had mentioned.

"Joe, why?"

"I didn't want to, man! I swear to you. Some guy hired Louie Balboni. Paid him to find a hit man to kill Dorrie, a contract killing, you F.B.I. types call it. I guess Louie was fresh out of hit men, plus he's keeping me as his crime slave because I owe him a ton of money. And then there was that little threat – either I do this or he'll kill me. But I couldn't do it – I certainly didn't want to do it – and I decided I definitely wasn't gonna do it! I thought if I just nicked her – make it look like I tried, you know? But then I realized Louie Balboni would kill me anyway for not doing it. So the only thing I could think of, was to turn myself in. I just really hope Dorrie is going to be okay. Is she — do you know? Please tell me she is."

"I think so. It looks like a flesh wound that just bled a lot."

"That's enough," Sean said. "Take him away – and make sure they have Louie Balboni picked up. Oh and one more thing. Protect this idiot. Don't let any of Balboni's men get to him. We're going to need him to testify against Balboni."

"Will do, Agent O'Hara."

Ben was itching to get back to the others.

"Sean. We've got to hurry. Cassie's missing! Come with me, I'll explain as we catch up to the others."

"Oh no," Sean screamed as he ran after Ben. "Please tell me it isn't true."

"I wish to goodness I could," Ben turned his head to say. "With all my heart I wish this wasn't true."

Sean quickly organized the officers and volunteers in a ground search. Halfway between the school building and the back of the booths, they found Cassie's pocketbook. She had taken it with her when she went to see Vicky, thinking she might want to buy a drink or something. The ground was churned up, showing signs of a struggle. Shirley, Cassie's Mom, started crying. Vicky, who had shown them the direction Cassie had gone, had stayed to help look. She walked over to Shirley and threw her arms around her.

It was obvious that Cassie had fought every step of the way to the parking lot.

"Why didn't she scream?" Ben asked.

"My guess is he held a knife or a gun to her and let her know he would use it if she opened her mouth," Sean answered.

Ben was sorry he asked.

When they got to the parking lot they

questioned everybody around.

There was one family sitting on a blanket having a picnic under a large maple tree near the parking lot.

When Sean questioned them, the woman said, "I saw them! I know because the girl was wearing a white polo top with that logo – Cassie's Cuisine. You see, I had two of those scrumptious seafood rolls of hers. In fact, I was going to go over and tell her how wonderful they tasted, but my husband said it looked like she and the man were in a hurry to leave so I didn't."

Sean felt sweat drip down his neck, collecting at his collar. Please, God, he prayed silently, let her have a description of the guy.

"Is everything okay?" the woman asked. "Didn't you say you were from the F.B.I.?"

"Yes Mam and I'm sorry to say that Cassie didn't go willingly with that man."

The woman gasped.

"Oh no! If only we'd gone over."

"Don't think that way Mam. If you had, he may have killed her or even one of you."

She turned white.

Way to go, Sean, he said to himself. Scare the witness.

Regaining her composure she said, "Agent, I think I can help. The man was tall and large. About the size of my brother which makes him 6'2" or

6'3". About one hundred-ninety pounds. He was wearing those army clothes – that olive green shirt and pants and no hat. His hair was salt and pepper – perhaps a touch more dark than light – but definitely mixed. Big ears. Thick, bushy beard but short. Also salt and pepper. Too far away to catch his eye color. Sorry. And they got into a VW camper bus. Also green."

Sean wanted to clap his hands.

"You're amazing, Mrs.?"

"Violet Maynard."

"Well, Mrs. Maynard, you have wonderful powers of observation. And you, Mr. Maynard?"

"I only watched for a few seconds, but Violet got it right – the part I saw anyway."

"By any chance did either of you see what he was wearing on his feet?"

"Oh – didn't I say?" Violet asked. "Black combat boots. Pretty worn, too. I'd say they were the real thing. In fact, everything about him – the slightly stealthy way he walked – the way he shifted his eyes all around – it just screamed 'veteran.' I remember thinking, poor man, he must have served in the war."

"Wow! That's incredible."

An officer had joined them and Sean directed him to get the Maynard's info and set up a time for them to come in and give their written statements.

"Okay, Ben and everybody. I've got to go put

out a BOLO, be-on-the-lookout, for the camper bus and I want to get a helicopter up to search a larger area. I'll keep in touch." And Sean took off running.

~~~~~~~~~~~~~~~~~

Across the Cape, on the north side near the water, in an old building, the doctor paced the cracked cement floor. Every few feet he stopped, ran his right hand through his greasy hair and sighed. Then he paced again. Over and over in his mind he tried various scenarios. But none of them ended up with him coming out on top. That was unacceptable. He'd been following directions. Hadn't he?

I'm not responsible for this mess. Face it man, this isn't a mess, this is a full blown catastrophe. On his feet he wore black leather shoes with black laces, and thick rubber soles. They squeaked on the floor. No matter how many ways he played it through his mind he didn't come up with an answer. He'd have to call him. Oh no, he thought. I really don't want to see him. Not only is he a certifiable nutcase masquerading as a doctor, at least, that was his opinion, but he could be quite vicious. That had taken him totally by surprise. I remember when I told him the subjects had adverse reactions to the drug and he asked me what kind of reactions. I told him they expressed a greater level of psychosis. He kept saying that will change when the drug gets into their system longer. But that's not what occurred. I told him to stop the experiment, it was getting too dangerous but he refused. So now, here we are in the midst of this mess that is about to blow up in our faces. Well, he better be right here when it does. I'm not going down alone for this. He started it and he can finish with it when they get him. It'll be a toss up as to who gets him first, the cops or the inmates. With a gut bellowing sigh, he picked up the phone and dialed.

The man himself answered.

"Hello?"

"Jameson, we've got problems."

"I thought I told you don't call me here."

"Screw that! You've got to get over here. He's escaped again! And the others are becoming more aggressive. I don't know what to do. To tell you the truth, I'm scared. I'm thinking about running. And what do I do with those other two? I've got them locked in a room."

"What did you do that for?" Jameson asked.

"Because I don't know what else to do with them! Look, you created this mess. Now come help me figure out what to do!"

"Calm down, Virgil. I'll be along shortly. Stay put."

Sean had been back at police headquarters just long enough to update personnel in their respective part of the search efforts. The helicopter had arrived and he was about to head out. Sean felt sure they'd be able to spot that camper from the air.

"Excuse me, Agent, this call is from the team you have following that guy Jameson. They say he's on the move, in a hurry."

Sean picked it up.

"What's happening?"

"This Jameson guy came running out of that Institute like he was on fire. He hopped into his Ford mustang and we're following him. Right now we're headed into East Dennis near the beach. Hang on."

Sean waited. He was anxious to get up in the air where he could see that camper, but this sounded important.

"Oh brother. Did you say you guys were going to follow a green VW camper bus? Because there's one here that almost side-swiped Mr. Jameson's car. They both seem to be headed toward the beach."

"Follow them. Stay on them! We'll be along in the chopper very soon."

~~~~~~~~~~~~~~~~

Cassie was more scared than she'd ever been in her life. This guy, with his hairy beard and long hair and scruffy look, she thought of him as The Gorilla. Plus he acted only semi-human.

He is definitely part of that evolutionary line descended straight from the apes. He is driving the camper with his right hand but holding the gun in his left and pointing it directly at me! Good thing it isn't slippery out, he's barely looked at the road. Just stares at me. And what is with those eyes? They're dark, almost indigo, shining like there is a fire burning beneath them.

The heat pouring out of the vent was suffocating. It was a dry heat and Cassie thought she might choke. It didn't help that the smell coming from him reminded her of wet dirt. Earthy and almost moldy. Where did that come from? At least he wasn't ranting at her. In fact, he spoke gibberish every now and then, sending shivers up and down her spine.

"Where's Eddie? Got to find Eddie." He kept muttering it over and over.

This man is behind the wheel? Are we going to crash? I haven't even been paying attention to where we are. I might as well see where we're going. It looks like either Brewster or East Dennis. The marsh is closing in on the road, and there's more sea grass here now. I'd say we're in East Dennis, very close to Cold Storage beach.

"Uh, I don't suppose you'd like to tell me where we're headed, would you?"

He grunted. "The place."

"Excuse me? What place?" she asked.

"Virgil's. You gotta stop him. And stop me before I hurt you. It's his fault. Or that other doctor's fault. They gave me those drugs. Totally make me nuts. Want to hurt someone. Want to kill!" he yelled, waving the gun at her.

"Whoa, soldier!"

"Don't you know anything? You yell, 'halt!' to a soldier. I'm not a freaking cowboy or a horse!"

"Sorry, uh, is it captain?"

He looked over at her. "Yeah, how did you know?"

"We studied the insignias in school."

"Oh. Yeah. Retired captain. Or discharged or something. Not right in the head. They didn't fix me. Made it worse."

"Are you sure?" Cassie was searching from the corner of her eyes. There was a stop sign up ahead. Maybe she could jump out. And then what? Run? I bet he runs fast. Much faster than me. But on the beach? Maybe I'd have a chance in the sand cause it would slow him down too.

He hadn't answered her.

"Captain? Are you sure the drugs aren't helping?"

The captain grabbed her arm and plowed through an intersection, ignoring the stop sign. They almost collided with another car.

"Can't take a chance you'll run. I told you – you have to get them to stop. They think they're helping the vets, the soldiers that come back broken, but they're making us worse. The doctor may have started off with the best intention – to take away the fears and the nightmares but there's something seriously wrong with the drug. It's been making us more aggressive and angry and still not taking away the horrific dreams – it doesn't take away the screams we hear in our sleep, the helplessness we feel when we relive seeing our buddies get killed. And where's Eddie? What did they do with Eddie?"

That long speech totally surprised her. She'd begun to think he couldn't form anything longer than a few words strung together.

"OOH," he started screaming.

"What's wrong?" she asked softly.

"My head," he yelled, putting his gun hand up to his head. "The pills give us headaches."

While the captain was grabbing onto his head, he probably didn't realize that the van was coasting to a stop. Looking furtively around she saw that they were in the parking lot of an old dilapidated building. Cassie glimpsed the ocean through the thick trees. The beach was around back. Just go for it – don't think about it, she told herself, just grab the door handle and yank it open.

"Stop!" he screamed.

So she ran, faster than she'd ever run before.

When the shot of his gun roared, Cassie felt the whip of what must have been sharp bits of gravel bouncing up, hitting her leg. Today had been so hot, Cassie had worn shorts and now she wished she had on long pants. Her leg stung like a swarm of bees was using it for target practice. Cassie started zigzagging, thinking it would be harder for him to hit her than if she was in a straight line. Now she felt warmth all over that leg. What was that about?

Cassie made it around the side of the building to the back. Praying she wouldn't slip on the sandy pavement, Cassie risked a look back. Darn, he was gaining on her, but at least he had put away his gun. That still wasn't comforting, remembering that Mary Chen's neck had been broken by someone's large, strong hands. Cassie had no doubt it was the captain, or the gorilla, who was right now closing in on her.

Huffing and puffing already, she jumped over the wooden railroad ties bordering the beach. The soft beach sand really sucked her feet down in, making it harder to lift them and run. *And WHAT IS that warm sensation on my leg?* Looking down, Cassie thought, uh-oh. Blood was pumping freely from a wound in her leg, running down and soaking her sneakers. Suddenly, Cassie realized that it hadn't been gravel that had cut her, but his bullet, probably grazing her leg. With blood loss, Cassie wondered how long she could keep running. Not to mention the furious pumping of her heart which was undoubtedly causing the blood to ooze out faster. As she was trying to think of a new strategy, one thing was clear, his superior strength had taken over and was propelling him faster toward her.

Before she could come up with a plan, Cassie heard the wump-wump of a helicopter. Sure enough, silhouetted against the blue-gray twilight sky, a helicopter appeared. After running full tilt on the sandy beach at dusk, with a maniac chasing her down trying to kill her, Cassie was beyond relief at seeing the helicopter hovering above them. She watched Sean O'Hara open the helicopter door and put his feet down on the runner. Oh Lord, don't tell me he's going to try and jump down from the helicopter, Cassie shook her head in disbelief. Then she saw his gun. Not only was it drawn, but he aimed it at the gorilla who had already caught up with her. They heard the whine of the shot over the rotors, much to her amazement. Should she look back and see if he was successful, or keep running in case he wasn't?

Sean signaled a thumbs up. Cassie stopped. She bent over trying to catch her breath, then slowly turned to face her attacker. With her chest heaving, gasping for breaths she couldn't get, Cassie thought she was going to faint. Lying practically at her feet, was the captain. A man imprisoned by his fears, then used as a guinea pig to test a drug that made him even more psychotic. That doctor, Cassie thought, should be charged with manslaughter just as the captain will be charged, if he lives. At that moment he was up on his knees, grunting while he tried to get back up.

Cassie was beginning to feel weak. She tried pressing her hands against the blood spurting from her leg, all the while trying desperately to stop the insane pumping of her heart. Well, maybe not all the way, but at least slow it down. The chopper lowered slowly to the beach where Sean and the others jumped out, running at her. Glad I'm on the side of the good guys, she decided. They grabbed hold of the captain and wrestled him to the ground, taking no chances, snapping the cuffs on him. It was over. It was really over. But Cassie couldn't enjoy it, she felt too close to passing out.

"Medic!" she heard someone scream. But after that, Cassie didn't remember much, just snatches of conversation here and there. It seemed too difficult to tune in and open her eyes so she kept them closed and slowly zoned down somewhere deep. Until at one point she heard a particularly insistent voice.

"Cassie!" the voice said, over and over. She eventually realized if she didn't make the effort to return to the surface and answer this jerk, he'd never leave her alone. So, Cassie made an all-out attempt, forcing her mind to focus and her eyes to open. It took immense effort but something inside her said, *it's time to come back.*

"Oh my darling, thank goodness!" Ben practically screamed. "Doctor," he screamed. "She's awake."

Cassie tried to reach out to him, but Ben had run out of the room to get a doctor.

When the doctor came in, he shooed everybody out. Cassie hadn't even realized that Ben wasn't the only one in her room. As they filed out, Cassie saw her Mom and Dad, and Gram, and sure enough, Janie snuck by the doctor and ran up and kissed her on the cheek. "We'll be right back," she whispered.

The doctor finished writing his notes and turned his attention to his patient. "Are you laughing, Miss Woods?"

"Who me? Maybe just a little. Don't you know that humor is good medicine, Doc?"

At that, he smiled.

"Well, you probably figured out by now that you were struck by a bullet. It was a bad graze. We had to give you more blood. The wound has been cleaned and stitched, but you won't be running on beaches or anywhere else for quite awhile. In time you'll have physical therapy, but until then you'll have to use crutches. Also I've started you on a course of antibiotics and we've had you on a morphine drip for the pain. That will continue for today then tomorrow we'll switch you to oral painkillers. Any questions?"

Sure, dozens, she thought, but none the doctor could answer. He left and they all came crowding back in.

"Okay, so who's going to tell me? What happened after I left?"

Ben walked over to the side of her bed and picked up her hand and held it.

"Believe it or not, none of us knows what went on. We've been waiting for Sean to get here and tell us."

"Did I hear my name mentioned?" Sean called from the doorway.

Everybody talked at once.

"Hold it!" he yelled. "Everyone get comfortable and I"ll tell you the story. But first, Cassie, how are you?"

"Good, Sean. My leg will be fine. There's a lot to do before I'm running around again, but at least I'll be able to."

"That's great news," he said.

"Okay, everyone get comfortable."

Ben pulled a chair up beside Cassie. Mom, Dad, and Gram sat in the only other chairs available. Janie and Kevin sat on the empty bed beside her.

"While we were capturing your attacker, I had men who had been following Jameson and they grabbed him when he pulled up at the building. By the time we got back up off the beach, a half a dozen cop cars had arrived and there were cops swarming all over the place like ants. Only someone had gotten there before us. There was a car we didn't recognize parked at the building."

Sean leaned back against the wall and folded his arms.

"My men and I started into the building, having no idea what we were going to find. It wasn't empty. In an office on the first floor, we found Kat Puskas holding a gun. She had it directed at the doctor."

"Which doctor?" Cassie and Jane shouted at the same time.

Laughing and shaking his head, Sean answered, "Dr. Virgil Mennin. He was sitting at a desk and she was standing over him with the gun."

"Hey Cassie – remember what Bonnie told us Kat's last name meant in Hungarian?"

Cassie shook her head no.

"Puska means gun."

"So why was she there? And why was she pointing a gun at Virgil?" Ben asked.

"Will you people please let me finish the story first?" Sean asked, exasperated. "As I was saying, Kat was trying to get Virgil to tell her where Christine was. She had followed him from his home earlier in the day and when they had ended up at the building, she decided to confront him. Kat thought by waving the gun at him that Virgil would tell her either where he was hiding Christine or what had happened to her. He hadn't gotten a chance to answer when we barged in. After I relieved Kat of her gun, I persuaded Virgil to tell us what was going on. He led us to a janitor's closet where he had locked inside, Christine White – and are you ready for this? – your friend, Gigi, Georgina Shepherd. Both of the gals are fine. Neither of them had been harmed in any way."

Every body clapped.

"That wasn't the only surprise we found. Virgil also led us down to the basement. We found small rooms, about the size of jail cells, all of them locked. Inside each one was a man. It turned out that they were all homeless vets taking part in Jameson's research experiment. You could tell right away that they had been drugged."

Cassie could tell that Sean was getting agitated. He began pacing the floor.

"Virgil told us about the experiments that they had been carrying out on these men. The drug that Dr. Jameson invented was supposed to help them overcome fear, but instead it caused them to become enraged. The men got to be so aggressive and in some cases, violent, that Virgil had begun to substitute valium for Jameson's drug, trying to calm them down."

Cassie asked, "Did the guy who took me – was he the one who killed Mary Chen?"

"We think so but we'll know more after I get to question him further."

"You mean he's still alive?" Cassie asked, feeling uneasy.

"Don't worry, he isn't in this hospital. We have him in a locked ward at Bridgewater – you know, the hospital for the criminally insane."

"What kind of drug did they give them at first to make them so nuts?" Janie asked.

"We're still not sure. Virgil didn't know what the drug was made from. The toxicology lab will analyze their blood and see if they can isolate the compounds. The good doctor Jameson wouldn't tell us."

"Jerk," Janie added.

"They were probably worse than jerks," Cassie pointed out. "I hope they're held accountable for whatever those poor soldiers have been through or whatever they might have done while they were under the influence of their designer drug."

"Don't worry, they will be charged with everything the U.S. Attorney can think of to throw at them," Sean assured them.

Everyone sat quiet a moment. The tension and fear of the last few days began slowly seeping from their minds and bodies. Winding down is a slow, cautious process. You're not quite ready to trust that everything is finally okay.

Cassie looked out the window. "It's dark out there. What time is it?"

"It's eight o'clock, honey," her Mom said.

"Then I want all of you to take off and go get something to eat. Most of you haven't been eating during this whole ordeal. Then, please, I want you all to do something for me. Go and watch the fireworks and relax. Now go!"

"Is it okay if I go home and sleep?" Gram asked.

"You bet."

She walked over and kissed her granddaughter goodnight. Gram's heart was filled with gratitude, for Cassie's rescue, for the safe return of those girls, and for getting that awful experiment revealed and shut down. There really is a lot to be grateful for, she thought, as she ushered the others toward the door.

Cassie started yawning as she said her goodbyes.

With the pain med kicking in, it feels so good to relax. It's been quite awhile since I last felt this relaxed and rested. Maybe this wasn't the best way to get it, but I might as well take advantage of it. But there's still a few questions nagging me. What were they? Oh, I remember.

"Sean?" Cassie called to him before he left.

"What's going to happen to Captain Gorilla? Will he just stay in that hospital?"

"Not exactly. The captain is being charged with murder. He claims he's never hurt anyone, that he never would, he saw too much of that in combat. I'm a trained investigator, Cassie, and I tell you it's odd. My personal point of view is that it has a ring of truth to it. From an investigative point of view it certainly points to him and only him."

"But couldn't Jameson's drug have made him do it? And who knows, maybe make him forget that he did it?"

"That's one of the things we have to figure out. For now he's being treated. Then we'll just have to see."

As Cassie yawned some more, Sean said, "I think it's time for us to leave. Cassie don't fight the drug, let it take you under for awhile. Your body needs rest to heal."

She nodded her head.

"But what about Joe Picoli?" she asked, remembering bits and pieces of the afternoon.

"He's been charged with assault with a deadly weapon. But between you and me, I think the D.A. is going to be looking for a deal – in exchange for his help in bringing down the Balboni crime family. Now rest."

The next time Cassie opened her eyes, the room was totally dark. All the lights had been turned out.

"Ben?"

"Right here, hon."

"What's that noise?"

"It's the fireworks. They started a few minutes

ago. We can see them right through your hospital window. Look over there," he pointed at the side window.

"Might as well climb up here beside me and get comfortable while we watch," she said, with twinkling eyes.

Ben joined her and they snuggled together, watching the light show that shined through their window just for them.

Fireworks exploded in the night sky, high above Lewis Bay. At anchor beneath them, small motorboats dotted the ocean, dwarfed beside the Tall Ships that came to the Cape as part of the Bicentennial celebrations.

Electrifying colors and shapes splashed against the darkness, lighting up her hospital room. Cassie couldn't believe she was lucky enough to be in one of the rooms that overlooked the bay, giving them front row seats to the biggest fireworks display in years. Suddenly the American flag appeared, impressionistic style, a blazing light from dozens of exploding fireworks. Ben and Cassie heard 'oohs and aahs' coming from next door. They weren't the only ones enjoying the colorful, noisy display.

When the nurse came in to check her vital signs, Cassie asked her, "What's tomorrow night's entertainment? It's going to be hard to top that one."

She laughed and replied, "I just hope all that

smoke — the aftermath hanging in the sky – doesn't come floating in the hospital rooms. We're going around checking windows now."

Ben dutifully went over and shut the window. The final display, a cacophony of lights and sounds ebbed into the night, leaving a trail of smoke behind. Our country was now officially two hundred years old.

Once the grand finale had finished, Ben and Cassie turned to each other and Ben picked up her hand. Holding it so gently, lightly stroking the top of her hand, he struggled for a moment searching for the right words.

"Cassie, when I first realized you were missing, I couldn't stop screaming and shaking and I never felt so helpless in all my life. You mean everything to me. To think that for even one moment that I could have lost you, terrified me to a depth I didn't know existed inside me."

Cassie was surprised to see tears forming in his eyes. His royal blue eyes, normally so brilliant and full of color, looked like a faded replica of the real thing. She put her hand up to his lips. He kissed it and held it to his cheek.

"I wish it hadn't taken something so major and horrifying to wake me up and ask myself, 'what are you waiting for?' Why haven't I told you all this before. How very much you mean to me and that I want to spend the rest of my life with you, if you'll have me. Cassandra Wood, will you marry me?"

Now Cassie started crying. She threw her arms around him, kissing him, burying her head in his shoulder. "Yes, Benjamin Thomas Franklin, you bet I will."

Holding each other, their breathing quieted and their hearts started pumping to the same beat.

CHAPTER EIGHT

Cassie was so happy to see daylight, the real thing, not just through her hospital window. The doctor had discharged her, with crutches, and she was going to be getting visits from a home nurse to change her wound every day for a week until the next doctor visit.

"It's almost like being let out of prison, Ben."

"Imagine, you were only in there a couple of days and already you developed cabin fever."

"What can I say? I'm a gal that likes to be on the go. Just hope I can get the hang of those crutches."

"I'll help."

"So, Ben, are we on our way to see Dr. Virgil Mennin?"

"Nope, not yet. Sean told us to wait at home for him to come and get us. He said the only way this would come about is if he goes with us. But in the meantime, we have one stop to make, then home where everyone has put together a nice big lunch for you. They are afraid you didn't get enough to eat in the hospital."

"They're right. Honestly, the food wasn't bad, but the portions they give you look like they'd feed a squirrel and that's it. I was always hungry."

~~~~~~~~~~~~~~~~~~~~

Cassie's unusual request to see Virgil came about after one interesting visit to her hospital room from Special Agent Sean O'Hara. He hadn't been quite himself that day. When Cassie asked how the investigation was going he mumbled that it slowed way down. He appeared to be discouraged. They weren't any closer to finding out who hired Louie Balboni to kill Dorrie or why. And they didn't have much of a case concerning Mary Chen either.

When Cassie replied that she thought Captain Gorilla did it, Sean had gotten almost angry. His real name is Jeff Greaves, he had said. Captain Jeff Greaves, Sean reiterated, disapprovingly. Totally surprised by his reaction, Cassie apologized immediately. Something had changed. She still remembered Sean's words.

"No, I am sorry," he said. "It's just that this young man risked his life for our country, then he comes home and is treated like this. These men deserve our respect and our help. I look around and all I see them getting is a cold shoulder and very little treatment or help. And they desperately need it."

"You're right, Sean. I really am sorry. Captain Greaves got a raw deal when he was picked for Jameson's experiment."

"Some experiment. The 'doctor' had picked these men up off the streets of Hyannis, said he would give them room and board if they would take part in an experiment that would help them and other soldiers. That was it. Nothing about the drug he'd be giving them or any safeguards. Where's the informed consent? There wasn't any. Even after the men started displaying symptoms of irrational behavior, increased agitation, and finally aggressive, and in some cases, violent behavior, Jameson still wouldn't stop. Virgil Mennin switched the drug on his own. He had begun to fear for these men and their sanity as well as being concerned about others, should they leave before they were weaned from the drug. Still, Jameson refused to stop. Virgil was trying to close down the experiment on his own."

"What happened, how did Captain Jeff Greaves escape?"

"Dr. Mennin says that he thought Jeff had gotten the drug out of his system and was going to assist him in getting the others free of it too. So he didn't lock Jeff up, and when Virgil was busy in another room, Jeff simply walked out and took Virgil's van."

"But was he still under the influence at that time?"

"*No one knows for sure but he still had some traces of it in his system when he was admitted to Bridgewater. Since then, at the hospital, they've been getting him straightened out. Those headaches he was having are gone. Captain Greaves still insists that he never hurt anyone, that he certainly didn't kill Mary Chen.*"

"*What about kidnapping me?*" she asked.

"*Jeff told me that he went to the fair that day looking for someone, the right person, he said, who would help him stop the doctors – Virgil and Jameson. He says when he saw you walking across the grass that day he just knew you were the right one. In your eyes he could see everything he was looking for – kindness, caring, openness, and compassion. He knew you were the one who could help.*"

"*I remember one conversation in the camper we had that he told me about wanting me to help stop them. And he kept mentioning someone named Eddie. Did he bring that up to you?*" Cassie asked.

"*Yes. He named every one of the veterans that took part in the project and one of the names he gave us was Eddie. When I pointed out to him that we didn't find anyone named Eddie when we searched the building, he said that Eddie had started out as part of the experiment. But about five days into it, he disappeared. Eddie had become loud and pushy and difficult after he was given their drug. And Jeff thinks that Virgil and Jameson did something to him."*

"Oh my gosh. What do you think?"

"We have proof. He's telling the truth. Virgil was keeping a meticulous private diary of the whole experiment. Even the damaging parts. At least up to a point."

Cassie's mouth dropped open. "Seriously? Then what happened to Eddie?"

"The only thing in the diary says that 'the subject named Eddie had an immediate and violent reaction to the drug, so much so that Dr. Jameson felt he needed to get him treatment and remove him from the project. Dr. Jameson took Eddie to the hospital, at least that is what he told me.' Further in the diary there's a notation, 'In view of further actions of Dr. Jameson's, I now wonder what exactly he did to the subject named Eddie. I'm afraid to ask, but I must know.' He never wrote another word in his diary after that. And now Virgil is afraid to talk. He's very fearful of retaliation. And for sure, the answer isn't going to come from Jameson, I know that much. He's clammed up, lawyered up and bailed out."

"Jeesh. What about Virgil?"

"Like I said, he's afraid, but I'm working on him."

"Sean, I know this is a bit unorthodox, but do

you think I could go with you when you talk to Virgil?"

"I don't see why not as long as there is someone else there to protect you, I guess it couldn't hurt."

~~~~~~~~~~~~~~~~~

So, Ben, what mysterious stop are we making before we go home and eat?"

"How do you feel about the beach? Did your experience with the captain affect your love of the ocean surf and sandy beach?"

Cassie hadn't thought about it yet. "Well, I'm not sure, but I don't think it'll bring back bad memories. Or if it does, they won't last. I love the water and beach too much."

"I'm glad to hear it," he said, driving them down the beach road in his bright red Triumph TR6 convertible. He worried at first whether Cassie would be comfortable, considering the injury to her leg. But the Triumph had plenty of leg room. It turned out that the crutches were the hard thing to fit inside the car, but he got it figured out. Ben pulled up and parked at the scenic spot where Bass River meets the Atlantic Ocean.

Sea gulls screeched overhead and they breathed in the fresh ocean breezes full of healthy, salt air. Cassie wondered at what point they would allow her to soak her leg in the salt water.

Ben took a small box from his pocket and opened it.

Inside Cassie saw the most exquisite pear-shaped diamond ring she could ever have imagined. In the bright sun, the dazzling stone reflected the brilliant light.

She threw her arms around him.

"Does that mean you like it?" he asked.

"I love it!"

Shortly after, they drove back to her house and Cassie couldn't wait to show her Mom and Gram her beautiful engagement ring. At least she was hoping they'd both be there for lunch.

It took a few tries and lots of help from Ben but she finally managed to get up the stairs with the crutches.

"I really thought you were a goner for a minute," Ben said, "you practically did a back flip down those porch stairs."

"Do you think these things are really necessary? I mean, can't I just hobble around?" she asked him.

"Don't give up yet. At least give it a few days, okay?"

Then he opened the front door for her. Cassie hefted herself over the threshold, and looked up as a chorus of voices yelled, "Surprise!"

"Wow!" she exclaimed, taking in the incredible scene. "Ben, you said all those cars out front were for an event Janie was catering here today."

"Honey, I didn't lie. You're the event!"

When no one was looking, Cassie took off her engagement ring and asked Ben to put it back in the box and take it up to her room. That news was for a more private time. Ben decided to hide it under her pillow.

After much laughter and gabbing, different ones came up to her at the table where they had plopped her down to sit. Gigi Shepherd threw her arms around her in a big hug. "Thank you so much Cassie for all that you did to help stop those guys."

"I didn't really do much, Gigi, except get myself kidnaped, like you. By the way, which one did kidnap you and do you know why?"

"As to who, I can tell you that guy they call Dr. Jameson. As to why, I still don't have a clue. He looks kind of familiar to me, but I haven't been able to figure out why yet."

It was a buffet style luncheon in the Conservatory with a large table set up for those who wanted to sit, like Cassie. She got to chat with so many – Alma Rogers, Vicky had come with her daughter Sandy, and Vicky's mother, Bea Willows, Claire Dinwoodie, and many others.

Janie came running in. "Cassie! It's Dorrie's Mom on the phone. Dorrie made it through surgery fantastic, and the surgeon says they got all of the tumor out of her head. He seemed puzzled by the fact that the tumor had shrunk some since the last cat scan, but he said it was perfect, nothing else was impacted by it. She's going to make a full recovery!"

Clapping and hoots and yells filled the room.

A little later, Kat Puskas came up to Cassie.

"Funny how things worked out. I wonder if anything would have been different if Dorrie had taken the job."

Cassie looked at her, "What are you talking about, Kat?"

Kat sat in the chair next to her. "Didn't you know? Dr. Jameson had interviewed Dorrie at the Institute one day. He had asked her to cater the awards event. For some reason, she decided to turn it down. He wasn't happy about it at all. Although I'm not sure why. What did it matter if she did it or you did? If she had, I wouldn't have talked to you and your staff and got you involved in this whole affair. See what I mean?"

"That is amazing," Cass agreed. But she wondered about Dorrie and what made her turn down the job. There would come a time when she could ask Dorrie. It was just another piece of the puzzle. Who knows, she thought, if we'll ever be able to put all the pieces of this puzzle together.

Cassie heard more noise and yelling, most of it coming from Janie. When she came tromping in the room, she had a death grip on some guy's arm and Bonnie had firm hold of the other arm.

"Look who we dragged in. Your stalker was stalking right outside our house!" Janie was still yelling.

The guy looked scared. Cassie couldn't help it, she started laughing.

"What's so funny?" Janie demanded.

"I'm sorry. Jane Jankowski, Bonnie Sarris, please meet Lenny Marek. And Lenny, what on earth have you been doing stalking me?"

"I'm so sorry, Cassie. I guess it did seem like I was stalking you, but I couldn't dig up enough courage to just come talk to you. I wanted to talk to you alone, so I kept trying to find you alone but you are ALWAYS with someone."

"Well, if you want to talk to me, you're going to have to do it in front of my friends. What is it?"

"Believe it or not, I just want to apologize. Ten years ago I acted like the biggest jerk. When you were trying to help find Bobbie, you asked for my help and I pushed you away and told you to leave me alone. I was grieving in my own way, the wrong way as it turned out. I started drinking then and never stopped until about six months ago. Now I'm in AA and they encourage us to make amends for past mistakes. So I just wanted to tell you how sorry I am for being a big jerk back then, and now," he smiled sheepishly.

"Uh, Janie, would you do me a favor and ask Vicky to come here?"

In a few minutes, Vicky Doyle aka Bobbie Avery, came waltzing in and turned the color of ocean-froth white. "Lenny?"

"Bobbie? Is that really you?"

He started weaving.

"Uh,oh, watch him folks, he might faint," Cassie warned.

Soon everyone was fine. Lenny was forgiven and although Cassie would have loved to stay with him and Vicky, catching up, Sean had arrived and it was time for Cassie and Ben to leave with him to go interview Virgil Mennin.

On the way to the doctor's house, Sean explained that he had a document with him for Virgil to sign. He'd tell them more about it when they got there.

Cassie had never met Dr. Mennin. She pictured a middle aged skinny guy with a crew cut, thick rimmed, black frame glasses, and a pocket protector in the breast pocket of his white shirt. She was thinking of Jerry Lewis as the nutty professor, but without the goofy expressions. And that he lived in an austere bachelor pad.

Instead, they drove up to a white, clapboard ranch house, with a freshly mowed green lawn, a seashell driveway and window boxes full of petunias.

The man greeting them at the door was the size of an NFL linebacker and the aroma of pipe tobacco emanated from him.

"Please come in," Dr. Mennin said quietly. "Please call me Virgil."

Sean made introductions. "Virgil, before we get started, I'd like to deal with the formalities if you don't mind. I have some paperwork here for you to read and sign."

Virgil led them into a combination living room/den. Ben and Cassie sat on the oversized, pale blue and rose plaid couch. Virgil sat in a chair that he obviously used all the time. Next to it was an end table, where his reading glasses, thin gold frames, sat and a floor lamp. Sean handed him a pile of papers.

"Will Mrs. Mennin be joining us?" Sean asked.

Virgil's brown eyes softened when he said, "No, June is out right now. Agent O'Hara in the interest of time, I presume you've read these papers, please just summarize the contents for me if you would."

Sean wasn't sure it was the best protocol for him to do that, but the doctor was going to get his own copies anyway. "Of course. It is your plea agreement. The District Attorney has agreed to probation in the form of community service that you will fulfill at your new destination. You and your wife will be relocated to a new city and provided with new identities and protection. In exchange you will reveal to us today, on tape, everything that took place from the moment you first heard about these experiments to the day you were picked up by the police. That will include all knowledge you have of Dr. Jameson, including conversations and actions by him that took place in anyway connected to this case. We will then have your report typed up, and you will go over it and sign it. Then you will both be relocated and you agree to come back to testify at any trial that may occur regarding this case, including against Dr. Jameson in any charges that may be leveled against him. Do you agree? If you do, please sign at the end where it's indicated."

"I agree," Virgil replied as he picked up a pen from the table and signed the appropriate places.

Afterwards he removed his glasses, sat back in his chair and proceeded to tell quite a tale.

"Some of this you will find difficult to believe, but I assure you what I am about to tell you is the whole truth."

Sean nodded. "Then please continue."

About four months ago, Dr. Jameson contacted the federal government regarding an idea he had for an experiment that would benefit soldiers. He said the benefit would be to soldiers going to war or those who had returned. In his grant application he spoke of a drug that he and another man developed – Dr. Jameson never gave me the man's name, you'll have to get that from his records – and that this drug would affect the part of the brain that controls our fear. Soldiers going to war would be less fearful and therefore more intimidating to the enemy." Virgil paused.

"Are you all right?" Sean asked. "Would you like some water?"

"No thanks, I'm fine." He wiggled around in his chair to get more comfortable. "Where was I. The soldiers – those returning from war tended to relive some of their more horrible experiences. They've been known to wake up with nightmares. So this drug would take care of that problem as well, according to Dr. Jameson. The government turned him down. You can read the letters for yourself. Do you need me to say anything more about them?"

Sean responded, "No, that's quite all right. We have those."

"Dr. Jameson felt that the drug and its applications were of such importance that he decided to go ahead with a clinical trial using money from the Institute. I asked him if that was legal and he assured me it was. I had no way of knowing if that was true or not, but I believed him, as he was the Director of the Institute. Then he told me he already had the test subjects picked out. Dr. Jameson ran a counseling group for veterans returning from the Vietnam war, and he was going to get volunteers from his group. It was then that he formally asked me if I would assist him in this research experiment. I admit that I had some misgivings about the drug and about doing the experiment in this way, but I knew him, and that meant he was going to do this whether I helped or not. I believed that if I became involved that I could make sure the men were treated fairly and would have medical attention if needed. I made that one of the stipulations of my joining him and he agreed."

Virgil had a melodic, soft voice and he held us rapt with his account.

"Next, Dr. Jameson said he had the perfect place to conduct the experiment and the men could live there as well. I was pretty horrified when I saw the building and its condition, but he said he would make sure that the men had all the comforts they needed. So one day he brought us all over there and I don't know if you saw the second floor, Agent, but there were bedrooms up there. The men stayed there at first and we gave them the drugs on the first floor and I held counseling sessions with them in that front room that resembled a living room. Do you remember?"

"Yes, I do. It actually looked quite cozy. Whatever happened to change things so drastically?"

"Sorry, but it's best if I tell this in the order that everything happened, if you don't mind. Otherwise I might accidentally leave something out."

"That's fine, please go on."

"So everyone settled in, and we had a nurse come in to administer the drug, it was injectable, and she came to do blood draws three times a week at first. Now I believe you've heard from Captain Greaves that one of the men had an immediate and violent reaction to the drug. Eddie Souza was the man's name. The nurse gave him a sedative and suggested to Dr. Jameson that he be cut from the experiment. But Dr. J said for her to give the man benedryl to counteract the allergic reaction. She tried to explain to him that this wasn't an allergic reaction but he wouldn't listen. He insisted that Eddie be given his dose of the new drug on three more occasions. Eddie continued to have even more violent episodes as time went on. He was the first one we had to lock up as the others weren't safe. Eddie wanted to kill all of us. On the fifth day, Dr. J arrived and said it was time for him to take Eddie to the emergency room at the hospital to be treated and he would be dropped from the project."

Virgil picked up his pipe and lit it. "Do any of you mind? It helps relax me."

We all shook our heads. Even though Cassie knew that any smoking was bad, the pipe had a pleasant aroma.

It took a few puffs to get it started.

"Things get a little hairy from this point on." He stopped a minute, thinking. "That's the wrong word. They get dangerous. I had no reason at that point to disbelieve Jameson when he told me he'd taken Eddie to the ER. It was about a week later when I asked him how Eddie was doing, that he told me what had happened. You won't believe it and I know you'll wonder why I didn't go to the authorities. The day that I asked about Eddie, he told me to stop asking. He said, 'Virgil you really are naive if you think I could just drop this man off at the ER and have them find my drug in his system. What do you think they would do to me?' I answered that I supposed they might take away his right to practice medicine. And I was thinking to myself that they probably should. So I asked him, what did you do with Eddie?" Virgil bowed his head a moment and sighed. "Jameson told me that Eddie had an epileptic fit and died. So early one evening Jameson rented a boat and took Eddie's body in a plastic bag and threw it in the boat and took off. About fifteen miles out in the ocean he dropped his body."

Cassie gasped.

"Oh, that isn't the worst of it," Virgil said. "I wish it was. Remember that young gal, Mary Chen? She had a part-time summer job working at the Hyannis marina, renting out boats. She had rented Dr. Jameson the boat that he had used. So he decided that she shouldn't be allowed to identify him. Jameson came back at closing time and strangled her."

"Oh my goodness!" Cassie screamed. "Sorry, Sean," she apologized for her outburst.

"That's all right. It's hard not to react to that.

Virgil, are you saying that Dr. Jameson murdered Mary Chen?"

"That's exactly what I'm saying. Then one night he took Captain Greaves' boots when he was asleep. He put them on himself, and apparently he had Mary's body in his car. Jameson drove over near Nickerson park, wearing Greaves' boots, carried her into the woods and buried her. Sorry, I forgot something. I have to back up a second. That girl, Georgina Shepherd? I believe she's called Gigi?"

Sean nodded.

"Do you know what her job is?"

"Yes, she works at Woolworth's at the Cape Cod Mall."

"Correct. In the hardware department to be exact. And Jameson needed a small shovel he could put in his car and take with him to the woods. He had to dig a shallow grave to bury Mary Chen."

"Oh, don't tell me. Because Ms. Shepherd sold him the shovel, he decided she had to go, too?" Sean's voice reached a new octave.

"You guessed it. He brought her to the building. This time he wanted me to do it. Jameson thought we could give her a drug that would put her to sleep permanently. I told him he was crazy and if he harmed one hair on her head I'd turn him in. By this time I wanted out of the whole thing anyway. He was getting crazier by the day and so were the men."

Cassie raised her hand.

"This isn't school, you don't have to do that, young lady. Please feel free to speak," Virgil said.

"Was Dr. Jameson always like this?"

"I don't even have to think about that. The answer is no. Most emphatically. It was this experiment that changed him."

"Really? Do you think it's possible he took some of his own drug? That he self-injected?" she asked. "And that's what changed his personality?"

Virgil took the pipe out of his mouth. "I had begun to suspect that myself. I even confronted him with it. Naturally he denied it, but I'm quite certain that he did. Can you have him tested, Agent O'Hara?"

"Yes, I'll contact the D.A. to get a court order." Sean made a note.

"At this time, the men in the project were all experiencing psychotic symptoms and I strongly urged Dr. Jameson to shut down the experiment. He refused. As I told you before, I stopped the drug injections and gave them valium. I realized later that it might not have been wise, not knowing how the two drugs would interact. I wasn't thinking clearly, I just wanted the men to stop having those awful headaches and violent tendencies."

Virgil put down his pipe. "I think there's some lemonade in the refrigerator, is it all right if I get us all some?"

"Why don't I do it," Cassie volunteered. Sean

thought it was a good idea and she headed to the kitchen.

Virgil was nice enough to wait until she came back with the drinks before continuing.

"So I had Gigi locked up in the janitor's closet, partly to protect her from the men and also from Dr. Jameson. He called me up one day and said, 'You can't hold onto her, we have to get rid of her. She knows too much.' Then I heard him yell, 'Who are you?' He told me he'd have to call me back."

He was quiet a few minutes, thinking and sipping his drink.

"I found out later that someone had come into his office and heard the last part of his conversation about doing away with the girl."

"Do you know who it was?" Sean asked.

Ben said, "I bet it was Dorrie St. John, there for her interview about the catering job."

"You're a smart man," Virgil replied. "That's exactly who it was."

"Oh no! You mean it was Dr. Jameson who hired Louie Balboni to find a hit man to kill Dorrie?" Cassie asked in horror and disbelief.

Virgil nodded. "Yes, I'm afraid so. As I said, I learned this much later.

"Well, what then happened to Christine White, your assistant?" Cassie asked.

"Chris was very concerned about my disappearance. That's right, I forgot to mention that

Dr. Jameson had insisted I tell no one where I was or what I was doing. My wife went to stay with her mother in Florida for a month. She just got back a few days ago. Christine wasn't satisfied with the answers Jameson was giving her about me, so she decided to search his desk to see if she could find out where I'd gone or what happened to me. She never really trusted him. Unfortunately, Jameson walked in while she was looking through his desk. So he brought her over to the building, too. Then he told me to take care of both she and Gigi, right away. Or he would. I was trying to think of a place to send them to hide while I figured out how to close everything down safely and get Jameson put away. That's when the captain escaped and you all came into the story."

A noise came from the kitchen. "June dear, is that you?" Virgil called toward the kitchen. "Why don't you join us?" He turned back to us. "Any questions, then?"

If he expected us to all talk at once he was mistaken. Stillness filled the room. And then – a scream shattered the silence. Dr. Jameson burst into the room. His eyes, shining black orbs, drilled into them. One hand held a scalpel against June's pale throat, his other hand held her tight against his body. She couldn't move. The slightest twitch could have caused him to slice her neck. Cassie looked at Virgil, his face blanched and his chest stopped moving; he was holding his breath. Her heartbeat started galloping.

"Hello everybody. Virgil, you and your lovely wife and I are going for a trip together. I noticed some rope in a closet in the kitchen. Go get it, and don't call anyone or do anything foolish. It wouldn't take much for me to sever your wife's jugular artery and you know I'll do it."

Virgil slowly rose from his chair. As he got near them, Jameson pulled June into the room, away from the hallway where they had been standing. In the second that Jameson was watching Virgil, Sean had pulled his gun that quickly. Cassie could see it in his hand behind his back. She thought if she distracted Jameson, it might give Sean a chance to make a move, hoping that was his intention.

"Dr. Jameson." Just as she hoped, he turned toward her. "Did you inject yourself with your special drug?"

He smirked. "Of course I did. I wanted to show the world how powerful and wonderful this drug..." BANG. Jameson flew backward and fortunately his arm didn't spasm. If it had, he might have cut June's throat as he dropped back. In fact, as he was shot in the head by Sean, Jameson dropped the scalpel.

Unexpectedly, Cassie started crying and Ben pulled her to him, holding her close in his arms.

Virgil came running from the kitchen and tightly grabbed hold of his wife. After making sure she was all right, he checked Jameson's vital signs.

Nothing. He was stone dead. And Virgil wasn't ashamed to say he was glad.

"Even if he had been under the influence of that drug, I still hold him responsible. He should've stopped taking it immediately when he saw the affects, not just on himself, but on the men. He knew better and yet chose to continue. So, yes, he's totally responsible for all the death he caused."

"Virgil," Sean said. "This may change everything now that he's dead. Obviously we can't charge a dead man. I'll hang onto these papers, and leave you your copies. I have to call the medical examiner to take away his body."

Other F.B.I. agents arrived and took Sean's gun as evidence. The afternoon wore on and Cassie eventually asked if she could go home. She was exhausted. It was only this morning that she had been released from the hospital and she was feeling the need of her pain medication.

Sean let them go and promised to update them tomorrow.

It was a quiet ride home. Cassie didn't feel too much like talking.

"Ben, when we get home will you go upstairs and get my ring?" she finally said.

"Of course, hon. What is it?"

"I need to feel alive."

At home, Cassie slid the key into the door and they quietly entered. It was only five o'clock in the afternoon but Cassie was exhausted. She could tell there wasn't much energy left.

Ben hurried up to her room and brought back her ring. Standing in the middle of the big kitchen, he took hold of her left hand and slipped the ring on her finger. "I hope you haven't changed your mind," he said softly.

Cassie, just about the same height as her intended, tilted her head and kissed him. "I can't wait to set the date. That will make it even more real for me."

"I don't know about you, but I wish it could be soon. The summer is so busy for us both, though. Should we pick a date in September?"

Together they checked the calendar and chose September 25th, right after the beginning of fall, their favorite time of year. Cassie circled it in red.

"I think I hear Janie's voice coming from Gram's kitchen. I'm going to head that way."

"Do you want me to come?"

"Thanks, hon, but this is a moment to share with my mother, grandmother, and my best friend. And don't worry about me tonight. Gram has set up a bed in her den for me to sleep until I can go up to the second floor on my own. Hopefully it won't be too long. The hard part will be getting Middy used to sleeping down here instead of in our nice comfortable bed. Hearing her name, the cat jumped off her window seat and joined them. Ben picked her up and Middy started purring.

"Well, there you have it. Middy approves of our engagement."

"Maybe we should get her a mini-tiara to wear for the wedding."

"Oh please, don't spoil her any more than she is," Cassie replied. Both of them recognized they were stalling, not wanting to part.

"Cassie, is that you dear?" Gram called from her kitchen.

They laughed and kissed goodnight. "I'll call you later tonight," Cassie promised.

With a smile as huge and wide as the river, Cassie hobbled on her crutches into Gram's kitchen. The three of them were seated at the little table. Without a word, Cassie put her left hand out in front of them.

"Wow!" Janie exclaimed. "It's about time, too."

"It's beautiful, dear," Shirley said, getting up and hugging her daughter.

"Do you have a date yet?" Gram asked.

Janie put on the coffeepot, Shirley got out the sandwiches and Gram went to get pens and paper. They were excited about the news and couldn't wait to get started.

"We have a party to plan!" Janie exclaimed.

THE END